"Are you Dr. Lazarus?" O'Niel asked.

From amid the clutter of the mine hospital, a rumpled woman looked up with sharp gray eyes.

"Yes," she said. "Take two aspirin and call me in the morning. That's a medical joke," she explained when his expression remained unchanged. "Are you the new marshal?"

"I am, and I'd like to talk with you for a minute. Yesterday a man deliberately went into the atmosphere without a pressure suit. A couple of days before that, another man cut open his suit . . . on purpose."

"It happens here."

"Why?"

"I don't know. It just happens here. I can't tell you why. Some people just can't take it here after a while."

"Did you do autopsies?" O'Niel demanded as she began walking away from him.

"No, the Company wanted the bodies shipped out quickly, in the first place. And, in the second place, when somebody exposes himself to zero-pressure atmosphere, there isn't a lot to inspect. In the third place, you're becoming a nuisance."

O'Niel pulled out a drawer, blocking her path through the laboratory.

"I know," he said. "But I would like a record of all incidents like these last two that have happened during the past six months. I would like it real soon or I just might kick your nasty ass all over this room. That's a marshal joke."

Also by Alan Dean Foster

Alien

Published by
WARNER BOOKS

OUTLAND

Novelization by
Alan Dean Foster

Based on the screenplay by
Peter Hyams

WARNER BOOKS

A Warner Communications Company

For Emery Morris of Shackleford County, Texas,
My favorite ex-sheriff,
Who would understand O'Niel. . . .

OUTLAND

I

Nearly everything had to be imported to Io, including love.

It wasn't a duty station that inspired fond memories among those who served there. The men and women imported to exploit its surface felt no affection for their temporary home. Merely to tolerate Io required real effort because human emotions and attitudes underwent drastic changes so far from the warm Earth, and rarely for the better.

Surely it hasn't changed me that much, O'Niel thought. Sure the past several years have been tough. He was used to places like Io, though. As used to them as any man could get.

He was lying in the bed in the darkened room, hands behind his head as he gazed upward. Nearby a digital clock glowed a soft, mocking green. The ceiling was a sooty black parodying the space that lay beyond, a dark veil mirroring the smaller domesticated shadows that populated the bedroom.

Usually O'Niel was able to concentrate fully on his job, but tonight the shadows had seeped into his head, to muddle and worry him. They buzzed his thoughts, little worries obscuring purpose, indecision and uncertainty mottling the color of the future.

It was a future tied tightly to the supple, silhouetted form that slept next to him. He rolled over and rested on an elbow as he stared at the familiar curves masked by the loose folds of the thin blanket.

Why can't I ever tell you all that I feel, he wondered? Do you know, Carol, how much I depend on you? How much I love you and Paulie? I know I'm not eloquent and I'm sure as hell no poet. But I'd be lost without you. I wish I was confident enough to wake you to tell you that.

It was cold outside, colder than most men could imagine, let alone would ever experience. Inside here, now, in this quiet bed it was warm and comfortable and reassuring. How nice it would be to have that feeling all the time instead of just for a few hours each day and during the unconsciousness of night!

That wasn't possible, he reminded himself. His was a cold job, one that matched the nature of Io's environment. Some day soon, perhaps. He promised himself, as he promised the woman sleeping alongside him. Just one more tour, Carol. Just one more.

He reached out and ran a hand along the curve of her hip, down the gentle swell of her side, up to her shoulder, the tips of his fingers touching lightly her cascading hair and then on to her cheek. At the touch she stirred lightly in her sleep.

So beautiful, he thought. Even when she's turned away from me, even when she's asleep, so beautiful. I can't lose her, can't risk it.

Definitely the last assignment. The Company and the rest of them could all go to Hell. Some things were more important than a lousy job.

A part of him was dimly aware that he'd said that before, only for resolution to slip stealthily away, for committment to vanish. But this time I'll mean it, he told himself, this time will be the last.

He touched her again, his hand moving lower, the heat of her bare back communicating like a mild shock through his fingers. She stirred again, pulled the blanket higher around her neck.

O'Niel turned away, closing his eyes. Slowly the shadows haunting his thoughts broke up and went away, to merge with the shadows that filled the bedroom, and he dropped into the light, infrequent sleep that was both trademark and necessity in his work . . . .

Mankind had pushed and kicked his frontiers beyond the confines of a single world, beyond his primordial bubble of air. He sent probes searching the moons of Neptune and burrowed deep beneath the surfaces of the Moon and Mars. He mined the floating wealth that drifted between the red planet and giant Jupiter.

All were harsh and bleak and dangerous. But of them all, none was worse than Io.

There was very little sky and what there was of it was black as the dark side of Pluto. Instead of sky, there was a Presence. Tourists might have found the Presence inspiring and beautiful and even awesome but tourists did not come to Io. Io was a place to work, and to do your best to survive.

The Presence took the form of a monstrous, bloated globe of banded yellow and orange hell. Long ago man had named it Jupiter, after the then king of his gods. Man's gods were transitory. Jupiter was not.

The men and women who toiled on Io made up other names for the giant planet, names equally colorful, often scabrous, sometimes scatalogical. To them it was nothing to admire. It constituted an inescapable reminder of the precariousness of their position and of the enormous distance between them and warm homes on Luna or Mars or Earth.

Its initial impact on new arrivals was always noted with interest by the experienced Ioites. There was an unwritten, informal test known as "degree of flinch" to which the shuttle station operators, the first to greet newcomers, always subjected them.

It is one thing to view Jupiter from the inside of a spacecraft, secure in the knowledge that powerful engines stand ready to push you safely clear of that tremendous gravity. It's quite another to step out of a shuttle into Io Station, glance upward through the transparent access corridor, and see billions of tons of mass floating just overhead, seemingly poised to obliterate you the way a man would an ant.

So the station crew would watch with interest to see how sharply and how often a new arrival would flinch away when first confronted with that psychologically devastating sight. The quicker and more extreme the flinch, the more often it occurred, then the less time that individual was likely to spend on Io.

Of course, if you'd signed a time contract, as most of the transient workers did, then you were stuck. You didn't break a contract with the Company.

There was one other test, usually applied later. The Jump Test. The Station crew assured newly arrived visitors that you could actually feel the pull of Jupiter's immense gravity out on Io's surface. Given Io's light gravity, they assured you, would enable a strong and careless jumper to leap so far off the surface that Jupiter's gravity would take over and suck you helplessly out into space.

And that would be the end, because as the workers of Io well knew, Hell wasn't red. Dante had it all wrong. Hell was yellow-orange, striped like the eyes of a dozen angry tigers, with one big, ugly red eye always glaring unwinkingly down on you.

A meteor, an ambling chunk of long-ago, had made the crater. More recently, mankind had made the mine that rested inside it. The mine was the reason for his continued presence in a place which actively discouraged it.

The explorers had come and touched down, raised their flags and made their speeches and gobbled their ounce of glory and moved on. Others had followed. They were not speech-makers. Most found nothing, but one tired group of bored searchers had made a discovery inside this particular crater—a discovery of more than passing interest.

What they found was a huge body of ore, a hard black mineral called Ilmenite, a product of Io's volcanic upheavals. Ilmenite happens to be the principal ore of a certain metal, titanium, which is used for, among other things, the skin of spaceships. The presence of Ilmenite in vast quantities on Io paid for a great deal of trouble, a number of deaths, and the eventual establishment of the mine.

It was a big mine, indicative of its importance to the vast international conglomerate that owned and operated it. It had gone up fast and would die with equal rapidity once the Ilmenite ran out. But at the moment it was a breathing, functioning entity. It lived.

The men and women who made it a temporary home called the time they were compelled to spend there by another name. The fecundity of the human vocabulary when confronted with isolation and hard work and danger is truly astonishing.

Like some lazy cephalopodian monster, the mine crawled up the sheer wall of the crater, stretching metal tentacles to its rim and dipping steel ovipositors deep into its bottom and flanks. From a distance the mine looked like the creation of an inspired cubist, a grand Christmas celebration of lights and glowing towers. Up close the illusion vanished and it became simply another tool.

Translucent tubes and accessways connected the major structures. The thin filaments of metal and plastic seemed barely strong enough to hold in the pressure of precious atmosphere that made life possible on Io. They cracked and leaked and were hastily patched with epoxies and welds. Great care was expended in those repairs, more so than was spent in the fixing of mining equipment. Broken machinery meant red ink. Broken accessways meant death.

The shadows of the actual mining area were sharper than its design, but it was efficient if not graceful. Scaffolding stretched over a hundred meters down the side of the crater wall. The lower levels were soaked in darkness. The scaffolding seemed too thin to hold men, let alone their heavy equipment. In that respect, the light gravity of Io was a blessing.

Jupiter hung suspended overhead and blackness swallowed the crater's bottom. With such numbing alternatives competing for his attention, it was easy for a man to concentrate wholeheartedly on his work.

The scaffolding was formed from a heavily oxidized metal whose orange hue matched that of Jupiter, an unintentional mimicry. Most of the men and women who crawled and swung like their ancestors from the struts and braces did not know the name of the metal that gave them support.

Of one thing they were pretty certain, however: the scaffolding contained little if any titanium. That precious metal was too valuable to be used simply to give support to a few expendable miners.

One year, they told you. Just one year of hard work and your duty tour was over and you could go home, rich and satisfied with a job well done. It didn't seem like so long when you signed the contract. One lousy year, for more money than most of them could hope to earn in five on Earth.

After a month, you began wondering if it was really such a good deal. After two, you wished you hadn't signed. After six, you didn't much care about the contract or anything else anymore. After nine, you found yourself counting the minutes remaining to your year instead of the days.

After eleven months you spent much of your time trying not to scream. You watched longingly each time the shuttle departed without you. If you'd been lucky enough to have survived eleven months, that is.

There was no graveyard, no boot hill on Io. Excavation was expensive, and the great gouges left in the Ilmenite didn't lend themselves to gravesites. The running joke was that if you died while on Io, the Company treated you to an all-expenses paid tour of the solar system, concluding with a one-way tour of the Sun. It wasn't much of a joke, but any humor was welcome at the mine.

They all carried little suns of their own, the miners did. Sun-powered suns, work lights of pure white powered by the huge solar concentrators. Those vast panels managed to draw energy even from the distant, tiny star called Sol. The work lights playing over the crater wall made the mine look as though it were being worked by fireflies.

On Earth, where it had been designed, the mining equipment had looked gigantic. Jupiter took care of that fast, as it reduced all matters of scale.

In the mine the gargantuan cranes and crawlers looked like toys. They scuttled over the shrinking rim and the crater sides like fat gray beetles, gnawing away at the rock while pumps and generators emitted hums none could hear. But you could feel their vibration through the feet and gloves of your environment suit.

The miners grew quite sensitive to vibration. If it stopped unexpectedly it might mean that some crawler operator had paused for a quickie with his codriver. Or it might mean an overhead drill had shattered. That meant run like hell for safe cover before the flying bits of steel and plastic came hunting for your suit.

Everyone had a buddy out in the mine. You watched out for him or her. If you didn't, they might not watch out for you. Then there'd be no one to warn you of the silently falling, sharp rock that could tear your suit, exploding you out through the hole, guts and blood flying in slow motion toward the crater floor so far below.

Crane or screwdriver, everything in the mine had a use. Even the colors of the environment suits had purpose, and nothing to do with aesthetics.

Crater miners wore yellow suits. Equipment drivers favored red, while maintenance personnel were always blue-clad. Management wore white. The last was the subject of many jokes among the other workers. There was no purity on Io, save for the blackness overhead.

Additional identification of a more personal nature was provided by the nametags stitch-welded to everyone's left breast pocket. To management the suit colors carried more mean-ing than the letters.

Experienced workers could be seen disdain-ing the elevators and jumping from one level to the next, ignoring the vast drop. In the light gravity, leaps of prodigious size were within the ability of the puniest worker.

The Jove-jockies, as the multiple-tour work-ers were called, delighted in testing the limits of their expanded athletic abilities. They horri-fied newcomers wtih jumps that teased death, pushing their safety tethers to the limit.

One legendary miner, a four-year old-timer by the name of Gomez, supposedly had made the jump into Jupiter's waiting gravitational field. He'd jumped so high so hard that his tether had busted. His fellow workers had gathered below to watch him soar upward to-ward a yellow-orange death. His last word had been "mierda!" spoken in the self-amazed drawl of his native home state of Chiapas.

His comrades had watched because that was all they could do. There were no ships sta-tioned at the mine, none which could have affected a rescue. There was only the shuttle, and it came but once a week.

Every so often a Jove-jockey would retell the story of Gomez, supplying his own details and embellishments. The new workers would listen, and deprecate, and then when they were alone would wonder if it had really happened.

They'd glance up at the roiling, awesome mass of Jupiter pressing down overhead, and shiver, and hurry back to their work. It was better to concentrate on the rock.

Each colored environment suit was a little world, crammed full of liquid food, water, atmosphere, and the babble of many conversations relayed over open channels.

On the ninth level brilliant white arc cutters lanced the rock, separating chunks of ore from the crater wall. One of the miners pushed off and floated up toward Level Ten. Everyone moved carefully, always conscious of his or her individual safety tether. They seemed to be moving through water, when they were actually moving through nothing.

In contrast to physical movements, conversation proceeded at a frenetic pace. Mine-talk was a time-worn buzz of rumor, commentary on the ancestry of the supervisors and foremen, ribald jokes, curses, complaints, and quips, all counterpointed with the grunts and wheezes of people striving harder with their muscles than their minds.

"No way," the man with the name WALTERS stenciled on his suit was grumbling softly. "I told them, no way they're gonna bring an automated vacuum loader in here. Cost too many jobs and besides, the old jockies would never let 'em get away with it."

His companion, a bucolic individual named Hughes, laughed derisively. The sound came hollowly over the suit intercom units and possessed a faint echo.

"Wanna bet? When they installed them on Fourteen and Twenty-three they said it was just a temporary experiment. Well, they're still in there, on both levels, puffin' away all by their damned robotic lonesomes. That's some temporary if you ask me." He flipped a null switch on his cutter, gesturing to Walters' left.

"Hand me that connector, will you? Arc's sputtering. I'd better go to a new line."

Walters turned, picked up a thin metal tube from a cluster and carefully placed it in Hughes' glove. His faceplate was partly fogged over. Perspiration dribbled down his cheeks and chin. In-suit perspiration produced a clammy, hot-moist sensation that one worker had likened to drowning in recently dipped sheep. The smell that went with it only served to intensify the analogy.

Perspiration did not endanger a worker, however. Therefore it did not warrant additional Company investment in upgrading and improving suit design. And if the workers didn't have the heat to complain about, so the reasoning went, they'd find something else to complain about, wouldn't they?

"What about Wooton?" Walters had returned to reducing his assigned section of wall, playing the cutter across the bare black rock with a skill that depended more on instinct now than forethought.

"He's the shop steward. What'd he say? Union going to do anything to stop those loaders being installed?"

"I'll tell you what he said. Zip." Hughes' cutter slashed a long vertical burn in the cliff face, a carbon-electro exclamation point. "That's exactly what he said when I asked him about it . . . total zip."

Walters shook his head to indicate his disgust, though the gesture did not translate well through his suit. "They're always trying to pull something. Fucking company. Like they don't make enough profit out of this hole as it is. They have to try to keep cutting corners, try and push some other poor schmuck out of a job."

"Yeah, well, it's a bunch of crap." Hughes made a rude noise over the intercom. "No way they can get away with it, no way. They got seven worker shifts on Fourteen and Twenty-three, ever since they installed those loaders. You know the by-laws as well as me. 'Eight workers for each shift.' In black and white, that's what it says. *Eight workers.*" His voice lowered.

"I knew the two who got replaced. Mariel and Dortmunder. Good people. It's a damned shame."

Walters' energy level rose a trifle. "Yeah, well, they want to get cute, we can get cute, too."

Hughes' cutter snapped off again and he looked across to his workmate. "You got something in mind?"

"Damn right. I'm sick of being pushed around. I'm gonna tell Wooton I want a meeting. Maybe what we need is a new shop steward. By-laws are by-laws or they ain't worth shit." He picked at several dials set into the left forearm of his suit but they were already shoved as far over as they'd go.

"Jesus, can't they regulate these suits? Minus a hundred seventy goddamn degrees out here and we broil our asses off." He looked past

Hughes to where a third cutter was working another section of cliff face.

"Ain't that right, Tarlow?" The other miner didn't reply. Walters grunted, turned disconsolately back to his own work. Mention of the men replaced by the autoloaders had made him more depressed than usual.

Tarlow turned off his arc cutter, carefully setting it down in its cradle. Hughes and Walters paid him no notice.

"Where's your other suit?" Hughes asked his friend.

"In the shop, where else? Said they'd have it fixed two days ago." He made a noise, hesitated, then swallowed. "Know the worst thing about these damn metal overcoats? You can't spit."

Hughes chuckled. "That depends on your personal hygiene factor, I suppose. Some do it anyway."

"Not me," Walters replied. "I'm not that far gone. But I wish they'd fix my spare."

"Don't blame the shop. They're always backed up."

"Yeah, that's right, they are. How come they never put any automated help in *there?*"

"Autoservs are for replacing people, not helping 'em." He peered closely at Walters' faceplate. "Hey, you really are getting hot in there, aren't you?"

"That's a clever observation."

"Put some mylar over the sensor. Translucent repair stuff, not the opaque. Does something to the heating coil, without fouling up the climate chip. You stay cooler and nothing's damaged."

"Really?" Walters was genuinely surprised.

"No, moron, I just made it up." The sarcasm passed quickly. "Yeah, it works. Some wall fracturer up on Top Level found it out by accident. Didn't report it in because the Company would forbid it."

"Why?"

Hughes grinned behind his faceplate. "Makes the suit draw more power. You know what the Company would think of *that*. The mylar fools the climate chip governor into thinking it's hotter outside than it really is, and so you get colder air. Most of the guys do it."

Walters shut off his cutter, moving to inspect Hughes' helmet. "Yeah, I see the stuff," he finally declared. "That's all there is to it?"

"That's all," Hughes replied, turning back to look at him. "Just make sure you peel it off before going back inside. Supervisor might catch it. Just throw the patch over the side. No problem getting mylar—it's all over the mine."

"Thanks," said Walters gratefully. "I can't wait for the next shift to try it out." They both laughed at that one.

The third cutter, Tarlow, stood shivering nearby while staring at the floor. He was mumbling something, but so softly that his words were lost in the static that filled the intercom channels.

"Ohhhhh . . . I hate spiders. Spiders . . . all . . . over . . . ." He started stamping on the metal platform, trying to smash something that wasn't there.

"Eight workers for eight jobs," Hughes was saying, having turned his attention back to the rock. "That's the contract Con-Amalgamated signed in order to get the mineral rights here.

They'd damn well better live up to it or there's gonna be trouble."

"Maybe our shop steward should read the contract. He sure as hell reads his paycheck entry before they put it through the computer into his account." Walters paused, stared past his friend and frowned.

"Hey, Tarlow," he called out, "what's eating you?"

The other cutter was now stamping and dancing with both feet. There was a hint of real terror in his squealing voice. "Kill it, kill it! For God's sake, don't let it get me!"

"Kill what?" Hughes had also turned around. "Don't let what get you, man?"

"Oh God . . . I hate spiders!"

"Spid . . . ." Walters looked uncertainly at Tarlow. "You shittin' us?" He glanced over at Hughes, who shook his head inside the helmet.

"Oh God, get it off my leg! It's on my leg. Get it off, get it offfff!"

Tarlow had ceased his stomping. Now he was flailing with both cumbersome arms at the right leg of his suit, pounding frantically at something only he could see.

"Tarlow, what's the matter with you? Get what off?" The humor was fading quickly from the situation as far as the other two miners were concerned.

"Spider! Please help me!" Tarlow, no longer groaning, was screaming now, his tone way up in the panic range.

"Spider?" Hughes was worried, but also mindful that Tarlow might be putting them on. The humor at the mine was usually as rough as the living conditions. Hughes had no desire to play the sucker for somebody else's crude idea of a practical joke.

"Have you popped your cork?" he asked the seemingly desperate miner. "How can there be a spider here? There's nothin' alive here and no bug's got a chance in hell of surviving all the multiple decontaminations all the way out from Earth."

"He's putting us on," Walters decided with assurance, turning back to his job.

Tarlow's frantic hands had worked upward and now were slapping at his chest. Behind the faceplate his eyes bulged in terror as something invisible approached them.

"Godddd. Get it offfffff!"

"Very funny, Tarlow." Hughes came to the conclusion that his friend was right. Tarlow was having a laugh at their expense. The act was badly overdone.

"We're not falling for nothing. Cut the garbage and get back to work. We've got a shift quota to fill, you know, and Walters and I ain't gonna make up no shortfall of yours."

Tarlow did not respond. He was suddenly grabbing at the base of his helmet, near his throat. His frantic screams were louder than ever.

"It's getting inside, it's getting inside!"

He was digging at his suit with a clumsy, heavily gloved hand, scratching and pawing at his left shoulder. "Get it outtttt! Oh Godddddd!"

Lurching forward he grabbed at a tool bin. Among other things the bin contained a brace of the fine-pointed carbon-alloy projector nozzles from which emerged the pure energy beam that ate away the Ilmenite. The point had to be needle-fine to insure proper focus. In a sense, it was a drill bit which never actually touched the rock it cut.

Tarlow pulled one out and started stabbing repeatedly at the shoulder of his suit. Hughes and Walters were suddenly awake.

Hughes lurched toward him, his own eyes going wide. "Holy . . . Tarlow, don't!"

They were too late. Lack of gravity defeated them, ironic as hell in the shadow of Jupiter.

The mine suits were tough enough to stand a lot of casual abuse, to turn the points of rocks and metal edges, to shield a man from a terribly hostile environment. They were not designed or intended to stand up against a deliberate, desperate attempt to defeat them by an andrenalin-energized man armed with a needle-pointed shaft of unbreakable metal.

The gash Tarlow made in his suit was above the shoulder and close to the base of his helmet, shearing through all four layers of suit material. What followed took about a second.

There was no pressure to speak of outside the suit. Hughes and Walters heard the terrible whoosh of escaping air over their intercoms, the death whistle every worker dreads will someday sound in his own ears.

The sudden rush of blood trying to burst out through restraining veins turned Tarlow's face crimson. Though he was already screaming, the sound didn't have time to emerge from his throat. Eyes exploded from their sockets to pulp against the inside of his faceplate. Red and gray mush erupted from the holes in his skull, filled the helmet with a moist syrup.

Some was already spewing from the tear in the suit.

The violent gush of escaping air and blood propelled the cutter's body backward and over the thin railing. In slow motion, the corpse tumbled toward the blackness that masked the crater's bottom.

It was still attached to its safety tether, which could do nothing to help its owner now. The suited body jerked to a stop, bounced at the end of the cable with a horribly animate parody of life. It hung there soundlessly at the end of the long green line, oozing a thick red fluid.

Hughes and Walters leaned over the railing, staring, the only sounds in their ears the steady babble of hundreds of other busy, still unknowing miners . . . .

II

Compared to the quarters of the average mine worker, those of the O'Niel's were luxurious. Nothing could be done to camouflage the exposed ventilation system piping, of course. It ran exposed beneath the low ceiling, thin conduits of life that supported everyone in the mine, a constant reminder of the tenuous hold oxygen-breathing life had staked on Io.

The walls were metal save where the warmth of pastel plastics had been used to mute the harshness and provide a little color. There were polyethylene plants and silk flowers, but no wood. Metal and plastic components could be manufactured nearby, in the zero-gee industries of the asteroid belt. Wood had to come all the way from the other side of the Universe, from Earth.

Still, there were a few hastily added attempts at hominess, attempts to conquer sterility with imagination. Beyond the bright silk flowers there were multi-hued chair covers, personal artifacts, framed photographs. And paint. Paint was a great humanizer of metal. It couldn't mask the ventilation pipes or circuit conduits, but it could soften the cold walls and force back the proximity of a hostile environment another few meters, if only in the mind.

There were two claustrophobic bedrooms, tiny compared to what was available on Earth but enormous in comparison to what was available to the average worker on Io. There was a separate, private bathroom that boasted a stall shower. The family room doubled as dining alcove, kitchen area, lounge, and work room.

Standard furniture would have filled all four rooms to capacity and left no room for inhabitants, but everything possible was built into the walls. None of the appliances were colored. Enameling was expensive. A millimeter-thick layer of enamel was weight, and weight transshipped to Io was money lost to the Company. The O'Niels didn't rate the extra millimeter, and couldn't afford to ship in their own appliances.

One wall was taken over by a pair of large video screens, a computer terminal, and a swarm of environmental controls and monitors. The fact that the room had its own environmental controls attested to the status of its occupants. Most of the workers tolerated the temperature and breathed the atmospheric mixture that the central monitoring computer saw fit to dish out.

A lean, dark-haired woman in her middle thirties was placing frozen waffles and a cup of coffee into a microwave oven. Her coiffure was a little too perfect, her attire a shade too trendy for her to blend properly with her surroundings. She didn't fit with the bare metal and exposed piping. One might say that she glowed with the extra millimeter of enameling that the rest of the room was missing. She was pretty, a raw sort of beauty. Once she'd been prettier still, but the past years had knocked all the edges off. The facets still gleamed, but they'd been battered and scratched.

She moved slowly around the room, a special kind of slowness which revealed that it was her mind and not her body that was tired. She leaked a kind of sadness of the spirit, a melancholy just perceptible enough to be noticed. What was really sad was that she felt the need to do her very best to conceal it.

Waiting on her with the usual impatience of any alert eleven-year-old was Paul O'Niel. His life was simpler and did not reflect his mother's fatigue, revolving as it did mostly around food and sleep, with occasional unpleasant intrusions by scolding and schooling.

His eyes were never still, hinting at burgeoning knowledge somewhere within. Too much knowledge, perhaps. The intelligence and quickness he displayed were promising. He also revealed considerable sophistication at times. Sophistication in an eleven-year-old is disconcerting.

Carol O'Niel noticed the anticipatory, hopeful stare. She sighed and managed to smile at him. "Be ready in two minutes, Paul. I promise."

"Is it the buttermilk kind?" The voice, at least, was open and guileless, devoid of the enforced maturity he'd acquired during the past two years. She was glad of that. He'd be grown soon enough. She knew what the frontier did to children, sending them directly from infancy to adolescence. *Do Not Pass Go, Do Not Collect Childhood.* She didn't want that for her son. She wanted him to be a boy, for a little while, at least.

"I'm afraid so," she answered.

"Yuck." Pure eleven-year-old response, that, she thought gratefully.

She turned away from him, from the table, pretended to study the readout ticking away on the oven. She did it so he couldn't see her face. It's awkward to have a son who can read adult expressions so clearly, she thought. That comes from associating primarily with adults. Also from learning to read eyes and mouths through transparent environment suit faceplates.

"I tried to get some of the maple-flavored," she told him apologetically, "but Supply said they ran out of them. The other flavors, too."

Eleven-year-old minds have the wonderful ability to switch from one subject to another without any hint of transition. Paul whistled as he spoke because his fingers were playing with his teeth.

"I can hardly talk with these braces, mom.

And the long-range broadcast when the Shuttle Tower's talking to the ships hurts my teeth."

"Now Paul, you know that's only your imagination," she chided him.

"S'not," he protested. "Anyway, I can't talk right. The Teaching Program hardly understands me during lessons."

"I know, I'm sorry." She turned a sympathetic smile back to him. "In any case, it won't be for too much longer, if the dental program says they've done their job."

He perked up, braces and buttermilk forgotten. "Really? How much longer?"

"Pretty soon." She ran fingers across her forehead, brushing back a strand of black.

"How soon?" they said simultaneously, Carol anticipating her son's next question and echoing him. He smiled up at her. He was such a bright, even-tempered boy, she mused. Hardly ever gave them any trouble, though he had a perfect right to. During the usual tests that preceded transfer, the doctor had called him one of the best adjusted pre-adolescents he'd ever seen.

But he was stifled by Io, she knew. Mentally as well as physically. Corridors and accessways were fine places for young rats to mature, not young men. Even the doctor's reluctant, encouraging smile hadn't been able to hide that fact from her.

"How soon for what?" a new, familiar voice wondered.

William Thomas O'Niel strode into the room. He always strode, never walked. Like a jogging thoroughbred, he was. Watching him you always had the feeling that he might break into a gallop at any moment. He moved with the loose, almost liquid motion of the natural athlete.

It was the stride of a man twenty years younger than his true age, graceful and unaffected. He was tall without being overbearing, though there was something about him that seemed too massive to be held in by chairs or rooms. It was a special quality that came not from his looks but from the way he regarded his surroundings.

His thinning hair was full of white and you had the feeling that there was meaning to each streak of silver. The lightness had crept down into the neatly trimmed beard he wore. Most of all he looked like a man who'd lived all his life outdoors, when exactly the opposite was true. His perceptions extended beyond his immediate surroundings, and it showed in his manner and his eyes.

It was a look common to all those who'd spent much time Outland.

"How soon 'til I get my braces off?" his son asked with a mix of anxiety and hope.

O'Niel didn't smile with just his lips. His whole face shifted slightly. An observer would get the feeling that this man had never learned how to smile properly. Or else something had made him forget.

He moved past the table to a small alcove like a shallow closet with no door and snapped on one of the video screens. He didn't have to look at the keys as he instinctively entered his personal call code.

"You want crooked teeth?"

"I don't mind them," Paul replied with the self-assured bravado that only an intelligent pre-adolescent can muster. He folded his arms, looked defiant.

"You're going to be missing some teeth in a minute if you don't eat your breakfast." O'Niel turned his attention back to confront the monitor. He'd punched for video response only, so it didn't talk to him. Few of the personal terminals on Io possessed that capacity. Voice circuitry was expensive.

PROCEED, it said in bright letters.

He entered the requisite response.

O'NIEL, W.T. ANY MESSAGES?

The monitor replied promptly: O'NIEL, W.T. AFFIRMATIVE. CONTAINS AUDIO. ORDERS?

O'Niel entered a reply. SUPPLY MESSAGES, VIDEO AND AUDIO. LOW VOLUME.

Carol left off watching him to respond to the gentle announcement from the oven. She opened the door and removed the contents.

Paul's eyes followed the buttermilk waffles as they descended like alien invaders toward his defenseless plate. They were already moist with something that might once have dreamed of a maple tree.

He stared at them, wishing his eyes were disintegrators, trying to make them vanish. They didn't. They just sat there, and waited, knowing they'd already won.

Carol sighed, tried her best coaxing manner. "Pretend they're not buttermilk."

He looked up at her. "Pretend I ate them."

"That's about enough pretending," she said,

a little more sharply. "You've had them before and liked them."

"Wanna bet?"

"Come on, young man. I know you can eat them if you put your mind to it."

He looked resigned and hefted his fork. "It's not my mind that gives me trouble. It's my stomach." He started picking at one of the waffles, using a technique best described as a desultory stab. His attitude was very like that the miners held regarding the rock they worked.

O'Niel had already speed-scanned his way through several routine messages. Now he caught a few words, rewound the tape and slowed the playback. He leaned back in his chair and crossed his arms as he studied the younger man speaking via the screen.

"Marshal, it's Lowell. The night shift went okay." From time to time the young deputy would glance down at the acrylic message board he carried to check himself.

What've we got? O'Niel asked himself silently. The taped figure was already responding, as though he'd been asked the question directly.

"Nothing much," the deputy said. He sounded bored. "Just a couple of drunks. Oh yeah, the door to the Purser's Office in Dome Nine has some chisel marks on the hinges. May have been an attempt to jimmy. No marks on the air lock, so it'd have to be somebody inside. Or it might be somebody just got bored and decided to devil us. We'll watch it tonight." He set the scanboard aside, stared out of the screen.

"That's about it. Real quiet. Just the way I like it." He grinned. "I'll be in the office at eighteen hundred. We can go over further surveillance possibilities on this possible break-in then, if you want."

Carol glanced over her husband's shoulder at the face of Lowell, which was winking off. She handed O'Niel his cup of coffee. He didn't ask her today whether or not it was real coffee, a running gag not only in their house but throughout the Mine. Hypotheses as to the origins of what passed for coffee throughout the Station generated an endless supply of speculations, some bizarre, few accurate.

A few tasteless folks suggested it was the one product that traveled through the Station's recycling systemology untouched, which would account for its strength if not its distinctive flavor.

On screen the image of Lowell was replaced by that of a heavier, older man.

"Montone here, Marshal. Got nothing more on that incident at the mine yesterday. Looks like it was just some guy who went whacko." The assistant marshal didn't sound especially interested. Death at the mine was nothing unique.

"The Company's having the body shipped back . . . or rather, what's left of it. Immediately, on today's shuttle. Guess they don't want the impressionable newcomers studying it. Can't say as I blame 'em." He made a face. "Christ, you should have seen the mess. They're shipping him back in a vacuum bottle, not a coffin. Don't want the remains leaking all over the rest of the cargo."

Paul had been having enough difficulty struggling with his waffle. At Montone's words a half-hearted forkful halted halfway to his mouth. He returned it carefully to his plate, his expression ample evidence that where eleven-year-olds were concerned, talk of bodies and buttermilk definitely did not go together.

Montone had paused, now rambled on. "Anyway, it's for sure no homicide. There were witnesses right next to him when it happened. Two guys saw the whole thing."

"Any witnesses to the witnessing?"

"I know what you're thinking, Marshal. Naw, they didn't cut his suit and push him over or anything. Couple of guys the next level down happened to be blabbing on the same suit frequency and heard the whole thing. Saw the last of it, too. Said the other two cutters were trying to help the guy who did it, there at the last.

"Spoke to both of the witnesses myself. They seemed genuinely broken up about it. At least, as much as anybody can get over a shift partner. They volunteered to take truth serum. I didn't think it was necessary."

"I agree," murmured O'Niel. "They volunteered, you say? You didn't suggest it?"

"Naw. Didn't have to. Figure that clears them, along with the testimony of the guys below who overheard it all." He went quiet for a moment, then shrugged as he continued.

"It just happens here every once in a while. I don't have to tell you that."

"No, you don't."

"Some people just let this place get to them." Montone chewed on his lower lip. "Damn shame, though. No reason for it. The guy . . . name was Tarlow, I think." He checked his scanboard. "Yeah, Tarlow. Damn shame. His year was almost up."

"What about an autopsy?"

Montone shook his head, looked regretful. "Impossible. I told you. Messy." He went down his board a last time.

"So, that's about it. Oh yeah. Tell your wife Transportation got the tickets for her that she wanted. See you when you get to the office. Don't worry. You'll get used to it. We all do, sooner or later."

He smiled perfunctorily. The screen blanked, read, END MESSAGES O'NIEL, W.T.

When Montone had mentioned "Transportation," what little color there was had faded from Carol O'Niel's face. She'd recovered her composure with admirable speed, however, if not for admirable reasons.

The Marshal stared a moment longer at the blank screen, expressionless. Then he reached out and flipped the monitor off. It died to black.

His attention on Montone, he hadn't seen his wife's momentary lapse. "What tickets?" he asked casually.

"Oh, Mr. and Ms. Reynolds," Carol told him easily as she worked at the dishes. "The nice couple from the bakery. They wanted tickets on the shuttle for a friend of theirs." She smiled tightly. "You know, they're low on the priority scale and so I said I'd see what I could do for them. It worked out fine."

"That was nice of you." He downed the last of his coffee. Or whatever it was. "I gotta go."

He rose, moved over to the central table.

His son didn't wince at the kiss, though the beard tickled his face, as always. "See you for dinner, sport. Don't forget. Seven frames of math. Two hundred through two-twenty on the tape."

Paul nodded. "I promise." He grinned slightly. "If the Teaching Program can understand my numbers."

"Braces bothering you again? Well, don't worry. It won't be for much longer. You don't want to grow up with crooked teeth, do you?"

"I don't see anybody else wearing them."

"That's because . . . ." He stopped himself. He'd been about to say, "that's because there aren't any other kids here." Instead, he said, "Because nobody else right near us needs them. You're just lucky.

"Anyway, the whole mine wears braces."

Paul looked uncertainly at him. "Huh?"

"Sure. You've seen those melted-in beams, the ones that rib the outer walls of all the buildings and the scaffolding for the heavy equipment?" Paul nodded, intrigued. "Well, those are the mine's braces, just like yours. Without them, all the walls would be crooked and weak. Just like your teeth would be if you stopped wearing them too soon."

"I guess I'd better keep them, then."

"I guess you'd better." He turned, starting for the door. "Don't forget that math."

"I won't, Dad."

Carol watched the byplay between father and son, fighting to keep a hold on her emotions. She rushed to intercept him at the doorway.

"You be good today," he told her, kissing her lightly. She pecked back at him.

"I will."

O'Niel was sensitive to many things. To movement, to eyes, to muscular changes in others. Little things. It was what made him so good at his job. He pushed her back a ways, and stared into her tired face.

"Look," he said softly, "I know this is a bleak assignment. I know what this is for you . . . how difficult. Just . . . give it a chance. It isn't so bad."

She stared back at him, searching his face, hiding feelings behind her eyes.

"I know. It's just that it's so, so . . . ." He waited. The words didn't, or couldn't, come. She finally gave up trying to articulate her feelings, shrugged helplessly.

He kissed her again, a comment far more soothing than any words, turned to leave.

"Bill?"

He looked back at her as she walked deliberately up to him, put both arms around his neck and kissed him again, fiercely this time.

"I love you."

"Well, I love you, too." He held her tight, smiled thinly. "Just give it a chance. We've only been here two weeks. It'll get better, I promise. Everything's unfamiliar and a little frightening at first in a new place. It's only for a year, and the pay . . . . you know what we made on the last job. That's one of the big reasons why I okayed this one. Just one more year, one year here and then, well, I might retire."

She leaned back, stared up at him and shook

her head once. "You'll never retire, not you, Bill. Not voluntarily, anyway. You like your work too much."

"Like it?" He laughed softly. "Hon, I don't like it much at all. But it *is* my job. It's what I do, and I take pride in doing it well."

You like it, she thought accusingly, but didn't say anything. Just held onto him and wished, wished that things were suddenly, magically different.

"I've got to go. You smell good." He touched her cheek with the back of his hand, ran it lightly over her still soft skin. She pressed it tight against her face.

Then he was gone. Carol moved into the doorway and stood there staring after him, seeing him turn down the corridor on his way to the next accessway.

In her mind she traveled outside the accessway, thought she could smell the pungent fumes that burst fitfully into the atmosphere from Io's interior. Sulfur and worse. There was atmosphere on Io, thin and sickly and unfit for anything living to breathe, atmosphere belched out by the unpredictable volcanoes that gradually bled away into space.

Lucky gases, she thought. She turned from the now empty corridor to check on her son . . . .

The cafeteria was huge, unattractive, and crowded. Workers exhibiting varying stages of fatigue shoved their trays down the long counter backed with pans full of steaming food. Like the tables and chairs that filled the floor, the counter was formed of unadorned gray metal or dull plastics. The light was harsh and even, pouring down from fluorescent slabs attached to the ceiling.

While the decor was subdued to the point of sterility, the richness of the conversation some-what made up for it. Clusters of miners swapped dirty jokes as they jostled through the long line or sat eating at individual tables, the peculiar confluence of food and sex as un-changed as it had been for thousands of years.

Many of the jokes were at least that old. Only the telling varied, the slang terms, the occasional references to weightlessness and canned air. Some of the female workers joined in these laughing groups with their male co-horts while others formed clusters of their own off toward the back of the room.

Isolated lumps of spice bottles and condi-ment containers littered the tables. As the food was generaly undistinguished and dull, these spices were provided to enable the workers to adjust the food to individual tastes, which were usually far more varied than the chef's menus. Meat loaf is meat loaf no matter where you find it, but salt and papper can make it taste one way and curry powder quite another. The con-tract workers at the mine were a polyglot lot.

The men and women continued to file through the entrance, pick up their trays, and shuffle into line. One man did not. He walked in and passed up his turn in line, heading for the eating area.

He was tall and lean, dark-haired and clean-shaven, in contrast to many of the bearded workers around him. His eyes were sunk more deeply than normal into the head and moved with purpose, as though their owner was constantly hunting for something. His hair was cut very short and was receding from the forehead.

He scanned the cafeteria, searching for something besides food. Eventually his gaze lit on a small, slim miner seated off to one side by himself whose attention eventually came round to the other's ... and passed on. Seemingly nothing had happened between them.

Several minutes went by. The worker at the table concluded some gratuitous conversation with another couple of men seated nearby. He put down his coffee, rose, stretched and headed unhurriedly for the back of the cafeteria, exiting through the rear door.

Another minute and the man with the deep-set eyes casually began to make his way through the noisy crowd, ignoring the occasional greeting or conversational gambit. Then he also left via the rear doorway.

Beyond the mess hall was the central locker room, a labyrinth of narrow aisles that formed canyons between endless ranks of high metal lockers. The benches, hangers, and storage cylinders were made of the same material as the tables and chairs in the cafeteria. The room's function might be different, the shapes altered, but all were born of some drifting chunk of nickel-iron halfway between Jupiter and Mars. It was sobering to think that some asteroid had waited billions of years, swimming in emptiness, only for an anthill of inventive bipeds to come along one day and turn it into, among other things, sewer pipe and clothes' hangers.

If anything, it was slightly quieter in the locker room than in the cafeteria. There was no food here to stimulate conversation. Also, the changing room was designed to facilitate business, not recreation.

Men were changing into or out of environment suits. Nearby the female miners had their own locker room.

Those slipping their suits on talked rapidly and with a nervous edge to their voices, trying to cover their anxiety at having to expose themselves once more to the surface of Io. Those taking suits off chattered rapidly and with a nervous edge in their voices to cover their feeling of relief at having completed yet another shift successfully.

There was barely enough room in the cramped confines of the aisles to manipulate the bulky suits but everyone managed. Here it was better to be small. You could move more easily and, outside, your emergency oxygen reserve would last longer if you ever had to use it.

The man who'd abandoned his coffee back in the cafeteria made his way down an empty aisle to his own locker. It took him seconds to activate the combination and the door clicked open.

Having accelerated through the back of the cafeteria, the dour-visaged worker who'd crossed eyes with him was barely seconds behind. They stood next to the gaping locker and chatted quietly, though one couldn't say amiably. There was an exchange of some kind.

Then the coffee sipper had slipped something into his locker and was climbing into his suit, preparatory to going Outside. His taller visitor had circled the far end of the aisle and was making his way back toward the cafeteria.

It all took only a few seconds . . . .

III

The worker's cafeteria was not the only place in the mine that served food. The other was nearby, but spiritually it was a light-minute away, and was barely a quarter the size of the cafeteria.

The tables were light and airy in design, giving the room an open feeling the claustrophobic cafeteria never enjoyed. There were napkins and formal table settings. One has to be familiar with interspatial shipping costs to realize the meaning of such mundane items as silverware and napkins on a place like Io.

The lighting did not waterfall down from directly overhead but was recessed, illuminating the Ward Room with a gentle glow.

There were even people to clean the tables.

At the moment some forty people occupied the room. They sipped at coffee (real coffee) or tea, or soda. There were two long tables joined to form a U-shape by a third. People sat on both sides of the long tables, chatting as they drank or smoked. A few glanced at the large readout which always kept tabs on the position of the weekly shuttle. The far end of the room was dominated by the massive company logo, a series of concentric circles that extended left and right in a rectangle, with the letters CON-AM inside.

At the far end of one table sat a man at first glance no different from any of the other occupants of the room. He was a bit larger than most and bald beneath the company cap. His beard and eyes were dark, his attitude seemingly indifferent.

His features seemed taken from a much smaller man, all squinched together in that falsely cherubic face, which gave all his expressions a forced look.

There was nothing of the athlete about him, but you still had the impression he was much faster than he looked. He gave off an aura of readiness. It was the look of a large fox. Or hyena, both equally dangerous when they wanted to be yet capable of controlling their ferocity.

At the moment the man was relaxed, a kind of tense tranquillity in his expression. His eyes moved lazily, studying the assemblage as it listened dutifully to the man standing next to him. The man was O'Niel, and he was doing something he was not particularly fond of: talking.

". . . finally," he was telling the crowd, "I realize that I'm still new here. You're going to have to get to know me, and I'm going to have to get to know you. There will likely be some times we won't see eye to eye. I hope few of them. I know we can work together and get along." He ventured a smile that was not returned.

"I just hope I can justify your confidence in me." He paused. The silence in the room matched the silence outside. The loudest sound came from coffee lapping against cup rims and one muffled cough.

"Thank you." O'Niel sat down. The quiet hung in the air like a fog.

He leaned over and whispered to the sergeant seated on his left. "I really wowed 'em."

"Had them eating out of your hand," Montone whispered back, grinning. "This is about as excited as they ever get at one of these things. Don't forget they'd all rather be shooting the bull and swapping gossip. This is their off-time."

"Are there any questions?" The query came from the bear of a man seated on O'Niel's right, who had finally bestirred himself. Sheppard never whispered and his question echoed around the room. He was never afraid of being the one to break the ice. If he so desired he could break much more than that.

A number of backsides shifted awkwardly in their seats. For all the talent and ability packed into the Ward Room, its occupants were acting like a bunch of schoolchildren waiting for someone else to tackle the teacher's question.

Finally an older woman raised her hand.

"Marshal . . . Flo Spector, Accounting Services." She looked around, as if seeking support
from her silent companions. "I'm sure I speak
for all of us here in extending our welcome to
you and your family. If there is anything Ms.
O'Niel or your son should need, please let them
know they can call on me. If I don't know the
answers to their questions, I'll know someone
who will."

O'Niel gave her a grateful smile, glad that at
least someone retained a semblance of neigh-
borliness. Of course, by the very nature of his
job he could hardly expect an outpouring of
affection. But he never got used to the cold-
ness, despite having gone through similar in-
troductory gatherings many times.

"Thank you very much, Ms. Spector. I will
be sure and tell Ms. O'Niel . . . and Paul."

He glanced around the room, searching for
signs of additional questions but there were
none. The boredom was plain on everyone's
face. They were ready to get back to work, to
relaxing, anything that would take them out of
the Ward Room and the unwelcome confronta-
tion.

Sheppard took over again. "Well, I see there
are no more questions." He looked over at
O'Niel, smiled. At least, it seemed like a smile.

"I would just like to add my welcome to
Marshal O'Niel. I'm sure you'll all agree he will
find this a pleasant and uneventful tour. I
know he's just started here. Io takes some getting used to, even for those of us who've put in
time at other Con-Am projects, but pretty soon
he'll find that this is just like every other mining town. There's never much trouble."

"I'm glad to hear it," O'Niel admitted. "I don't like trouble."

Montone shifted in his seat, looking the other way as Sheppard continued. "Just remember, these men and women work hard. Very hard. I'm proud of that dedication and I do my best to see that it's encouraged.

"Since I've been General Manager here this mine has broken all productivity records. We're on our way to becoming Con-Amalgamate's leading deep-system operation, and everyone in this room has received the bonus checks to prove it. There isn't another mine or manufacturing facility outside Mars that can boast our profit margin. I expect it to continue that way.

"Good work only comes from contented people." This time the smile seemed less forced. "I work them hard and I let them play hard."

O'Niel didn't respond to the subsequent pause, simply continued watching Sheppard. The manager gave a mental shrug and continued.

"So when the time comes to let off a little steam, you have to allow them some room. Considering how hard they push themselves out there,"—he jerked a thumb toward a port that showed the yellow orange surface of Io— "they're entitled to that." He leaned forward toward O'Niel.

"Just give them a little room." He was still smiling. "Do you understand what I'm saying, Marshal?"

There was an uncomfortable moment of total silence in the room. Montone wished fervently he was somewhere else.

He needn't have worried. O'Niel's response was noncommital but satisfactory. "Thank you for the advice, Mr. Sheppard."

"We're all professionals here," the General Manager added, relaxing in his chair.

"I'm sure we are."

"You drop around to my office." Sheppard was feeling quite content now. "We'll talk some more."

"I'll do that." O'Niel stood. "I'd better be getting back to the office." People were already filing out of the room. No one came forward to shake O'Niel's hand or wish him well. It didn't surprise O'Niel. He was used to that. "We professionals have our work to do."

"Right." Sheppard didn't rise along with him, signaled to a younger man to bring him some more coffee.

Once safely outside and halfway down a corridor, O'Niel let his anger out. Not by punching one of the prefab metal walls, or kicking at the unscuffable floor, or spewing a stream of curses. His face tightened a little, but most of the anger came out in his stride, which increased in length and force until his boots were hitting the floor with far more energy than was necessary just to carry a man forward.

They entered the vacuum-hose accessway which swayed under his march as Montone struggled to keep pace with his boss.

"Now don't go getting your nose all out of joint," the sergeant urged him.

O'Niel didn't reply, didn't slacken his pace. His eyes stared straight ahead, ignoring the dim light that flashed occasionally from readouts on the ceiling.

"What the hell was that all about?" he finally asked. His voice changed as he mimicked Sheppard's. " 'Do you understand what I'm saying, Marshal?' "

"That's just his way." Montone's voice was soothing. "A little ceremony for the good folk, that's all. I'm told he goes through that with every Marshal who comes here. He wasn't singling you out or anything like that. It's just his way. You know how some of these General Managers are."

"I don't like his way," said O'Niel softly.

Montone turned serious. "Not many people do. Only those who count, like the members of the Con-Am General Board. He gets results, Sheppard does. That's all they want to know. Don't mess with him."

"He's an asshole."

"He's a very powerful asshole. Don't mess with him! Save it for the rowdies in the Club. Take it out on them and stay away from Sheppard."

They walked the rest of the way in silence.

Eventually the corridor ended in a hatch seal. O'Niel thumbed the switch and the hatchway admitted them to Building C. The mine complex was full of hatches, double and triple checks to contain any accidental air leaks.

The combination switch on this particular hatch was unusual. Most such portals had only a single stud to press to gain the supplicant admission. But Building C was tighter: it housed, among other important sections, the security area.

There was a jail uniquely suited to its environment. Also separate artificial gravity con-

trols, a small squad–meeting room, a data
center far more sophisticated than the simple
double terminal in O'Niel's or anyone else's
living quarters, an interrogation room, and a
couple of small individual offices with glass
walls that overlooked the squad area.

On a door leading into one of these offices
was the legend:

FEDERAL DISTRICT MARSHAL
W.T. O'NIEL

The two men entered the security complex,
Montone still trailing his superior.

"He's just trying to sniff you out." Montone
was more willing to chat in the privacy of the
jail chambers. "The last Marshal before you
kept things running pretty smoothly. That's all
he wants—all *they* want.

"If things run smooth, they make their money and everybody's happy. Nobody's here for
their health or the scenery. Don't worry about
the ship's heading is what I'm trying to say.
Just see that she doesn't turn over and you'll
find everyone here warming to you real fast.
Not Sheppard; he doesn't warm up to anybody.
But the stone faces in the Ward Room, they'll
melt. They're just not sure of you yet."

They entered the squad room where several
younger deputies were seated. They stood
when O'Niel entered. He ignored them, march-
ing on past.

Possibly he just didn't notice them. His
thoughts were elsewhere as he entered his office, closing the door quietly behind him.

There were reports to check, information to peruse, duty rosters to okay and a number of other things he badly wanted to go over to better familiarize himself with the physical layout of the mine. He wanted to study them in private, so he could simmer unobserved.

One of the younger deputies glanced through the transparent wall at the silently working O'Niel and spoke to Montone.

"What's your opinion of this one, sergeant?"

"O'Niel?" Montone joined the deputy in regarding the new Marshal. "Too early to tell. Quiet, private. Not the sort you'd invite over for a game of cards. Not antisocial or anything like that. Just . . . quiet." He turned away from examining his new boss, looking down at the deputy's computer readout.

"That's about enough psychoanalyzing. What've we got that's new on that Purser Office business?"

The miner's name was Cane. He was a thin blond man decorated with an equally slim beard that gave him the look of a newly anointed bishop. His eyes were a pale, faded blue. Hair, eyes, and physiognomy marked his ancestry as Scandinavian, but that meant nothing to anyone on polyglot Io. It never mattered where you were from, who your people were, what you used to be. It only mattered how you did your job.

At the moment Cane's face shone with an expression of serenity that bordered on the beatific: his mouth was curved 'round in a little boyish half-smile that gave him the appearance of having just spent a week in the harem of a Turkish pasha and he wasn't about to tell anyone about it.

It was still light Outside. The locker room was nearly deserted, the day shift having concluded their work and the night shift already out on the job, save for a few stragglers. No one confronted Cane as he strolled smilingly down the aisles.

At the far end of the locker room was the spacious assembly area with curving steel tubes, like the horns of a dozen ferrous longhorns, that projected outward from a wall. Suits and helmets had been placed on these supports and awaited their owners. At the far side was a sealed, double-thick hatchway door lined with controls and admonitions.

On the door itself a legend proclaimed boldly: CAUTION — ZERO ATMOSPHERE BEYOND — PRESSURE SUITS AND OXYGEN REQUIRED

Cane leaned forward, his hands held easily behind his back as he peered through the single port into the airlock. It was empty, brightly lit. At his practised command the hatch opened softly and he stepped inside. After a casual survey of the walls he directed the hatch to seal.

It required several switches to insure that the hatch produced an airtight seal. The delicate nature of living on Io demanded that anything involving air be controlled by several backups. Cane was very thorough. When he was positive he'd carried out the prescribed procedure properly he turned his attention to another row of buttons, pressed one.

There was a soft whine behind the door on

his right, signalling that the mine elevator was starting upward toward his position.

A small group of men and women had finished topping off and checking out their air supplies. They'd donned the suits hanging in wait for them and were moving toward the hatchway, helmets in hand.

The usual joking and complaining ceased when one of them happened to glance curiously through the hatchway port to see Cane standing inside the sealed lock. It wasn't Cane's presence inside that cancelled the laughter: it was the fact that he wasn't wearing a suit.

They started pounding on the door and shouting.

From inside, Cane noticed the movements and smiled placidly back at them. He'd turned the airlock speaker off, preventing their frantic yells from reaching him. Not that anything they could have said would have made a difference. He might have listened, but he wouldn't have heard.

The other miners continued to beat on the door and port. The muffled shouts and pounding penetrated the lock to the point where Cane decided it might be nice if he responded. So he grinned at them and waved.

A buzzer sounded, heralding the arrival of the elevator. The thick door slid open and Cane stepped leisurely inside. He bestowed a final smile on the distorted faces gesticulating at him from behind the port. The smile was temporarily interrupted while the lift door slid shut, became visible once more through the elevator's port.

Inside, Cane studied the panel a moment before finally selecting a button and pushing it in. Nice button, he thought. Nice elevator, too.

From the other side of the airlock hatch the miners watched helplessly as Cane's face sank out of view. The elevator was on its way down. There wasn't a damn thing they could do about it, since the call controls were inside the airlock and that had been sealed from the inside.

One of them had the bright idea of calling Energy Central in the hope of having the elevator's power cut off. A friend reluctantly reminded him that the lifts were independently powered to provide service in case of emergency. The irony of that passed all of them.

"Damn, I'm beat," the tall driller declared, his voice echoing through his buddies' suit speakers. His hand came up and brushed lightly over his helmet faceplate. "Wish they'd figure out a way to let you wipe your nose in these things."

"That'll be the day," another tired worker snorted. "It'd mean they'd have to add another servo arm inside. Be glad they designed 'em to give you food and water."

"Food?" Another worker let out a derisive guffaw. "You call the mush they let you suck through these face tubes *food?*"

They shuffled about, impatient to be on their way upward. Their shifts had ended some ten minutes ago. Each moment spent in their suits was a moment lost, another minute of real life wasted. A minute when they could be eating *real* food, relaxing in the *real* air of the rec room or Club instead of standing around smelling their own recycled sweat.

So they waited resentfully while the elevator dropped patiently down to pick them up. The counter light set in the wall next to the elevator door marked its progress. Lights flashed on as the lift passed through ATMOSPHERE, travelled past GROUND LEVEL, DECOMPRESSION, NO ATMOSPHERE and thence to FIRST LEVEL, SUB ONE, SUB TWO, SUB THREE. It slowed and at last the SUB FOUR light winked beckoningly at them.

The elevator came to a halt. Red paint or something had been smeared across the port. Somebody's idea of a gag. The door slid aside

When what was inside became visible, the waiting cluster of workers forgot their intial impatience and made time to be sick . . . .

O'Niel was tired. It was amazing how exhausting ensuring the security of a small isolated community like the mine could make one.

Keeping a place like Io running smoothly was like riding a rollercoaster carrying a thermos full of nitro. You had to be able to anticipate the bumps and dips and react to them before you reached them. If you didn't they could swing you the wrong way and blow you right off the track.

So he apologized to no one including himself for feeling tired. He expected that. But at last the day's work was done and he could go off shift.

The door to the apartment slid aside, admitting him. He glanced around in the subdued light—everything appeared undisturbed. It was quiet, peaceful in the apartment. His haven. He welcomed it.

As he strode in and the door shut obediently behind him his brow furrowed. It was very quiet.

"Paul?" There was no joyful, high-pitched response, no glad cry of "daddy!" The only sound in the apartment came from the almost imperceptible whisper of the air cycler.

"Hey, Paulie?" He hesitated, called, "Carol?"

He waited for a long moment, now hoping for rather than expecting a response. A quick check showed that there was no one hiding in the bedroom, either. Well, hell, maybe they'd gone off to visit someone. He remembered the invitation extended by the older woman during his formal introduction to the mine hierarchy . . . Spector, Ms. Spector it'd been. Perhaps she'd given Carol a call and she and Paul had gone off to make some friends. No children, though. Outpost colonies like Io didn't favor children.

That thought started him worrying.

They could be anywhere. Maybe Carol had simply taken Paul shopping. There were very few concessionaires on Io, like the private bakery, but they always offered a welcome diversion to miners and administrators alike. Sure, they'd gone shopping, he decided. He could hardly blame them.

Meanwhile, he might as well check in case something had come in while he'd been out. He returned to the living room area, gave it one final look to make sure they weren't hiding in wait to surprise him, then approached the video monitor and activated the computer board. He stood and punched in his code.

PROCEED

He typed without looking at the keyboard.

O'NIEL, W.T. MESSAGES?

O'NIEL, W.T. AFFIRMATIVE, the machine declared.

He flicked the transmit switch and the screen came to life. The first face to appear was Carol's, which he'd hoped for. He knew she wouldn't go off before he came home without letting him know what she was up to.

Her expression threw him, however. She seemed on the brink of crying, sniffling, constantly looking away from the pickup, fighting back something struggling to get out.

"I . . . I'm trying to keep my composure," she told him, "and like everything else I do . . . I think I'm messing this up." She took a deep breath and the half-smile on her face twisted even further.

"I despise these message things. They make this kind of thing too easy. It's just that . . . I'm just such a coward. You know that. I couldn't stand there in person face to face with you and say what I'm about to say. What I've got to say. I just couldn't.

"If you were in front of me right now, I would change my mind. And I don't want to change my mind." There was another pause while she sniffled into a tissue.

O'Niel felt behind him for the chair, pulled it in under and sat down slowly. His eyes never left the screen. What was it Montone had told him? Something he'd hardly paid any attention to, wasn't it?

"You'll get used to it . . . we all do." Yeah,

that's what the sergeant had said. He'd ignored it. Those things happened to somebody else, not to him.

"I love you," Carol's distant voice was saying. "Please know that." Another uncomfortable pause while she dabbed at her eyes with the tissue. "I hadn't planned this. I really hadn't." She leaned toward him.

"Look at me. I'm asking for approval. My analysis tapes say I constantly crave approval, and look at me." She blew her nose, looked around, skyward, down at her feet, not really seeing anything, hardly daring to face him even via the mask provided by the video lens.

"Oh God . . . I just can't take it anymore. That's really what it comes down to. We've gone over this so many times before. We've had the same crying from me and the same assurances from you that the next place will be different. Well, this is the next place and it isn't different, Bill. It's never different. It can't be, except to be worse." Her eyes turned back toward the pickup and she was staring hard at him once again.

"So something snapped in me yesterday. I couldn't bear to watch Paulie clattering around still another bleak place. He has no friends. Ever since he was born he's been trucked off from one cesspool to the next, a year or two at a time. He's a child, and he's never set foot on Earth. Never. He reads and looks at pictures of Earth all day long, and then he hides them from you, blanking the recall code, so your feelings won't be hurt."

She smiled bleakly. "You know what he talks about all the time? Trees. Not Africa or sports or rockets or games. Trees. He's never seen a goddamn tree, Bill.

"But he's like his father. No matter how bad he's feeling, no matter how bad it gets for him, he never complains. He's not like his mother, God knows."

O'Niel leaned forward, rested his chin on his folded hands, his face lit by the glow from the screen. His muscles were all tight, belying his relaxed posture.

"Don't you see," Carol went on, "he deserves a childhood. A real childhood, before he grows up. He deserves a chance to breathe air. *Real* outside unrecycled air, someplace where you won't broil or freeze or explode. Air that smells like life, not like ventilation unit lubricant.

"You think it's all worth it. You think that you go where they send you. You keep the good old peace and do the good old job. Well, I'm not as fortunate as you. I don't have your abiding faith in whatever-it-is." The long-restrained bitterness was finally creeping into her voice.

"I can't see that, Bill. I can't see anything except one God-forsaken mining town that looks just like every other one. The Company is the *same*, the greedy people are the *same*, the violence is the *same*. I'm just not as good as you are. I don't think it's all worth it."

O'Niel's teeth had tightened against each other, until the small muscles in his jaw had started to twitch.

Carol was not quite finished. Her tone softened a little. "So . . . so I'm taking Paulie back home. Back to the home he's never had, back to the home he deserves. A *real* home.

"I love you, Bill. You don't deserve this. You deserve the best. I just have to go, my love. I'll get back in touch in a few days."

She stared straight into the pickup, evidently trying to add something else. She couldn't get it out. Her eyes were blurred and the tears had started dribbling listlessly down her cheeks. She swallowed, tried vainly to smile, and finally gave up, ending it with a pathetic little shrug, the mute gesture a poor substitute for the words she'd searched for unsuccessfully.

The screen blanked. Writing appeared, coldly indifferent.

END MESSAGES O'NIEL, W.T.

It blinked on and off, signaling silently. O'Niel ignored it, made no move to switch the screen off. He just sat there, gazing at the steadily blinking letters, his eyes staring but not seeing . . . .

Montone was running the regular morning roll call and check. The roll call really wasn't necessary, more formality than anything else. If someone was absent from duty, it was simple enough to check out their whereabouts as there weren't many other places to go.

O'Niel sat off by himself at the back of the squad room, partially taking note of what was being said and mostly someplace else.

"Okay," the sergeant was saying briskly, "what do we have?" He studied his acrylic board, then looked up toward one of the junior officers. "Ballard, what's happened with the Purser's Area? That was your job, wasn't it?"

The younger man nodded. "We've had a monitor on the whole section for thirty-six hours. It's been quiet as a church. Foot patrol turned up nothing either. No fingerprints when we went through and photographed, no skin oil residue around the jimmy marks, no body odor pickup. Nothing."

"Suits me fine," was Montone's opinion. "Keep the monitor on it for two weeks and discontinue the foot patrol. Maybe whoever did it has been scared off by all the attention. You sure the monitor's well hidden?"

Ballard nodded once more. "It'd take somebody with instrumentation to find it. I set it up myself."

"Good." O'Niel was chewing on a stylus, paying no attention to what was being said. Montone looked away from the Marshal, turning his attention to a more serious item.

"Nelson, what about the detonators?"

"They were found," the deputy in question informed him.

"Where?"

"I don't know." He looked unconcerned. "The shift foreman for the level they disappeared from reported that they'd been found . . . and said not to bother about it any more."

"Nelson, we're talking about nuclear detonators. You don't lose them and then find them. You lose your comb and then find it. But not detonators. I'm glad they've turned up, but that's not good enough.

"I want to know where they were found, who found them, and if there was anyone else around when they were found. You get my drift?" He stared meaningfully at the deputy.

"Yes, sergeant." Nelson's alertness level had abruptly risen fifty percent.

"Good for you, Nelson." Montone's gaze went back to the board. "What about the Club?"

"Nothing unusual." The deputy pushed at her hair, looked throughtful. "The usual junk. Oh yeah, Sheppard asked us for a couple more people for the late shift. You know, just to keep the boys and girls in line after a few belts. Seems they've been getting a smidgen rowdier than usual and he thought a show of force would be enough to get the troublemakers to tone it down."

"He can have them," said Montone agreeably. His attention shifted to the next in line. "Slater, what about the incident in the mine elevator?"

"Nothing much to tell, Sarge." The deputy made a face. "Some cupcake named Cane decided he wanted to go for a walk without an environment suit. They're still sponging him off the elevator walls. Couple of the off-shift people who greeted the remains got green enough to have to go on Sick Leave. Legit, according to the medics. Can't say I blame 'em. Helluva thing to run into unexpectedly."

Slater said it all matter-of-factly, without emotion, yet still managed something none of his colleagues had succeeded in doing: he woke up O'Niel.

The Marshal's gaze returned from the distant something it had been focused on to settle fixedly on the deputy. Other than that there was nothing to hint that he'd even heard the questioning.

"Any details?" Montone wanted to know.

"Not much." Slater consulted his memory. "He was alone. Nobody was near enough to have thrown him in. A bunch of the guys tried to get into the airlock after him, but he'd sealed it from inside. They were close enough that they would have seen anybody if he'd been pushed.

"Besides, the couple who got a look at him before he went downside and inside-out said he didn't have the look of somebody who'd been forced into doing something against his will. Said he was smiling all the time, right up to and including when the elevator started down. No way it could have been homicide. Had to have been suicide.

"Even if he'd somehow been shoved in he could have stopped the elevator anytime before passing Decompression. I checked. The controls were still on manual and nobody'd tampered with them. He didn't stop himself."

"Did he leave a note?"

The sudden presence of O'Niel's voice startled everyone. The Marshal spoke evenly, almost quietly, and yet he had their attention at once. It was a peculiarly confident voice, all the more arresting because its owner was now evidently interested in something.

"I beg your pardon, Sir?"

O'Niel repeated the question for the deputy. "I said, did he leave any kind of note?"

"Uh . . ." Slater was thinking fast and trying not to say anything stupid. "None that we know of, Sir."

"Did anyone think to look?"

Slater looked around for help. Another depu-

ty answered. "I was with him when we did the
report, Sir. I checked Cane's locker and quarters but there was no note, nothing on his personal computer line. He didn't say anything to
anyone beforehand, either. At least, not to any
of the people we talked to. If he said anything
to anyone else they haven't come forward with
it."

O'Niel looked back at Slater. "Then how do
you know it was suicide?"

"Uh . . . it . . . there's no other possible explanation," Slater said haltingly. "He knew exactly
what he was doing, that's for sure. You can't
fall into an airlock and then an elevator. You
have to open hatches, press buttons, seal
hatches, call the elevator, seal it, and chose a
level. All manually. None of those controls
were preset. That's so this kind of thing can't
happen accidentally. Suicide's just . . . the only
explanation."

O'Niel studied the deputy for a long moment, finally said softly, "Thank you."

"Yes, Sir." Slater no longer looked bored and
indifferent. Neither did any of his formerly
somnolent companions. They were all sitting
alertly now, trying to watch O'Niel without
catching his eye. The result was a flurry of
surreptitious glances that reminded him of a
bunch of respectable businessmen passing a
porno palace.

When it was clear that O'Niel was finished,
at least for the moment, Montone looked back
to his list. "Okay then, that's it for the elevator
business. Fanning, your turn."

Another deputy shifted in his seat, trying not

to look off to his left to see if the Marshal was watching him, too.

"What do you have on the pump station?"

"Just a fight. We brought 'em both in to cool off. They were straightened out in about an hour, shook hands, and went back to work arm-in-arm." Somebody made a rude joke, snickered, shut up fast at a look from the sergeant.

"Hill?"

"Pretty quiet elsewhere, Sarge. There were a couple of calls from the Administration residential level about noise in the corridors. Somebody reported a few viewing tapes stolen sometime last night."

"Probably left them in a drawer someplace."

Hill nodded then smiled. "That was my thought also, but I took the complaint just the same."

"Good boy. I don't need Admin on my neck about trivialities." He pressed a small stud set in the side of the board. Words rushed past through the acrylic surface, eventually slowed to a halt at the preset point.

"Duty roster for today. Fanning, it's your turn on Admin." The deputy so designated rose, started for the door. "Slater, you take the Club. Morton, you're on mine patrol Outside." She groaned.

One by one the deputies acknowledged their assignments and filed out. O'Niel watched them go, trying to grade them according to their reports but still thinking primarily of Carol and Paulie, and the distance that was growing between them every day. Both kinds of distance.

But there was also something else. It nagged and pestered and made a part of his brain itch. It wouldn't go away no matter what kinds of arguments he threw at it. He made himself a promise to scratch it further . . . .

IV

The bunks were multi-tiered and set in long aisles. Each bunk was home to the man or woman who slept there, the only home any worker could know on Io.

The people and computers who'd designed the bunks were interested in efficiency, the conservation of space, and not much else. Their creations reflected this. They offered their tenants enough room to stretch out in and to sit up and not much else.

One side was heavily screened to provide more security and a sense of privacy. Each bunk also boasted solid screens that could be closed to provide further privacy. Both ends of a bunk were solid, as was the overhead, and were insulated against noise as much as possi-

ble. That could inhibit but never eliminate the
dormitory feeling.

At least the beds were comfortable. They
had to be, since so much time was spent on
them. Drawers and cabinets were ingeniously
set into the headboard and footboard of each
bunk. Some of the workers had put in little
additions of their own, like portable drawers
magnetically secured to the sides of the bunk
or to the solid ceiling above. Along with food,
water, and air, space was not allowed to go to
waste on Io.

At the end of each aisle were communal
banks of video monitors. One provided a hundred twenty-three different entertainment
channels from classical music (which wasn't
much employed) to news (moreso) to porn
(less so than you might think) to sports (the
most popular by far) with every available
taped form of entertainment filling the channels in between.

Another monitor offered the time, not only
on Io but at over a hundred similar mining or
outpost stations as well as on Mars, Luna, and
Earth and the various deep-space support stations. It also displayed internal and external
temperature.

The internal readings were always carefully
discussed while no one paid much attention to
the external, since it never fell within the narrow band acceptable for human life. The same
was true of the readings for atmosphere.

Another screen offered tectonic information
and predictions. It connected to those outlying
instruments which kept a constant watch on
Io's unstable bowels and to the section of the

main computer which ventured forth predictions of upcoming I-quake and volcanic eruptions.

It also frequently put out short programs exhorting the miners to greater efforts. This Company propaganda was always ignored, as were most of the glowing fiscal reports. The only time attention was paid to the latter was when some mention was made of bonuses. Then the screen drew considerable attention, with everyone in the locker room trying to pack around their designated monitor.

These quarters were rarely entirely deserted. Someone was usually around, studying the screens, reading on private portable monitors or from a real book, changing clothes, sleeping with a closed bunk shield. Groups of men were leaving their bunks and going to and from the shower and bathrooms. The quarters for the women workers backed onto the hygienic facilities and were no different in look or feel from the somewhat larger male-populated dormitory, save for a slightly higher concentration of pastel decoration and the occasional bouquet of artificial flowers taped to the outside of a bunk.

It was impossible to navigate one's way down an aisle without having to squeeze past at least one or two neighbors. This crowding did not generate the mental discomfort early psychological planners had feared.

After all, sailors had been doing it on submarines for many pre-space decades. For that matter the entire Japanese nation had coped with such problems throughout history. It wasn't difficult. You created a little invisible bubble of privacy around you. No one intruded on it and you didn't intrude on anybody else's. A fair number of the Jove-jockies were of Japanese ancestry. The mine wasn't comfortable, but it worked.

It had to work.

The man with the broken nose who'd visited the cafeteria without eating on the previous morning now entered the locker area. He paused at the head of an aisle to glance above the heads of several other workers, at the screen they were currently watching.

It showed the replay of a recent major-league nullball game. The men muttered quietly to each other, occasionally letting out a curse or compliment depending on the play at the time, offering comments on strategy as they cheered the players and derided the referees.

After several minutes during which he joined in the conversation, Spota moved on down the long aisle. Ahead, a miner settled on the fourth, uppermost tier of bunks, swung his legs over the side and started to climb down. He reached the floor a few seconds after Spota passed beneath him.

Keeping some twenty feet apart, the two men walked the length of the aisle, ignoring other workers as assiduously as they did each other, and finally entered the bathroom.

Steam filled much of the large chamber, steam from recycled wash water that provided one of the few real luxuries for the workers. Loud voices echoed off the walls. Drenched, soapy men moved about in the open shower area, careful never to come in contact with the exposed pipes carrying the hot water. Other workers groomed themselves in front of mirrors.

The waste stalls were located near the far side of the chamber. Spota entered one, closed the door carefully behind him.

A few seconds later the man who'd left his bunk occupied the stall next to him. There was the usual wait, then he reemerged and left. Shortly afterward, Spota came out and headed for the exit. The worker returned to his bunk, Spota to an aisle leading out of the dormitory via an accessway different from the one he'd entered by.

They drew the attention of no one, which was exactly what they wanted.

The hospital was cleaner than the workers' dorms but far more cluttered, despite the built-ins and space-saving devices. The instrumentational overkill was necessary. The modest medical section had to serve the entire mine as dispensary, infirmary, emergency room, surgery, pharmacy, laboratory, and diagnostic center.

It was not patterned after the advanced, gleaming clinics found in similar locales on Earth. This was a place for repairing, not rebuilding. For fixing up, not researching. Its nearest analog at the mine was not the workers' quarters but the engineering shed where important mine machinery was patched up. It was no secret that the machine repairs were usually more permanent than those performed on the workers.

That was the hospital's primary function: to keep the mine's organic components operating.

Its duties beyond that were quite limited, reflected both in its equipment and personnel.

It had a full-time staff of eight, whose importance was secondary to that of the diagnostic machines. The staff was aware of their position in the medical hierarchy and it didn't bother them. On the contrary, they were glad of it. It was much easier to let the machines make the important decisions.

There were four nurses, three paramedics, and Dr. Marian L. Lazarus, who was sick of jokes about rising from the dead.

To new arrivals she was a figure ripe for fun, an easy target. They got the word quickly— don't joke with Lazarus. You just might find yourself in the infirmary some day with a busted leg or worse, and the last joke would be on you. The doctor was not noted for a tolerant sense of humor.

Lazarus was a rumpled older woman whose expression could shift rapidly from that found in a Goya war etching to the bright face of an alert twelve-year-old. The former predominated. Her eyes were gray and belonged to someone much prettier, which she had once been.

Her clothing was less disciplined than her hair. She looked sloppy in her hospital fatigues. Somehow she gave the impression that nothing ever excited her.

Her own personal bailiwick was located at the back of the hospital section. Despite the inherent efficiency of the built-in equipment and self-contained beds, she'd managed to personalize her area with bits and pieces of what could be described as medicated rubble. Garbage traditionally is one of the anthropologist's most useful tools for telling us what the people of a particular culture were like. Lazarus's lab table and the area immediately around it were very descriptive.

O'Niel walked into the hospital, past the admiring stare of the admitting nurse. His gaze flicked left and right, taking note of the state of the equipment and the other workers, a sick man in a bed, and the fact that the area was at least clean.

He had a special interest in hospitals, having had occasion in the course of his work to make use of their facilities. Sometimes personally, far more often because recalcitrant visitors to his own section usually spent some time making use of medical services prior to extended stays as his guests.

The equipment, insofar as he could tell, was up to date and reasonably well maintained. There was plenty of it, expensive and hard to ship. Pity the Company didn't devote as much care to its employees before they got hurt, he thought.

He found Lazarus at her private station, hunched over a stack of acrylic readout boards and a computer screen full of graphs and chemical symbols. At that moment, she was dividing her attention between the screen and a nearby nurse who appeared upset.

"Who the hell ordered all these pressure packs?" the doctor demanded irately. "Doesn't anybody have any sense around here? This is a mine we're responsible for, not a war."

"You did, Doctor." The nurse tried and failed to keep the irritation out of her voice.

"I said one hundred, not one thousand."

"You said one thou . . . ."

"I said one *hundred.*" There was enough acid in her voice to cut through stainless. "Which can't be mistaken for anything except one hundred. It doesn't sound remotely like one thousand." She looked up from the screen, slowed her words to a sarcastic drawl.

"Listen, you'll see what I mean. One *thouuuusssaaaand.* One *huuuundrrrreeedd.* They're totally different, aren't they? Not even close." She looked over a shoulder, saw O'Niel standing patiently behind her.

"You think they sound the same?" Then she frowned. "Who are you, anyway?"

"Are you Dr. Lazarus?"

"Yes. Take two aspirin and call me in the morning. That's a medical joke." Her eyes roved over him, noting the insignia on his jacket and the bars on his collar. "You're the new Marshal, whatsisname."

"Yes, I'm whatsisname. I'd like to talk to you for a few minutes."

"I got an alibi. I got four people who will swear they were playing poker with me." She didn't smile as she rose from the seat facing the screen and started for the small laboratory, having forgotten the nurse and the pressure packs. O'Niel moved around the computer terminal, smiled slightly at the put-upon nurse's see-what-you're-going-to-have-to-deal-with look, and followed the doctor as she made her way past tables and wall benches.

"I've never heard that one before," he murmured. "That's really funny."

"Sorry." Lazarus didn't sound like she was.

"Yesterday a man deliberately went into Outside without a pressure suit."

She lifted a bottle, checked the contents, set it back on the table. "Yeah, I know."

She was taking an inventory as she walked, matching readings on her board with various items in racks and cabinets. O'Niel didn't enjoy trailing after her as he talked. He didn't like conversing with somebody's back.

"A couple of days before that," he continued, "another man cut open his suit while working Outside. On purpose, it would seem."

Lazarus shrugged, didn't turn to look back at him. "It happens here."

"How often?"

"I don't know." She was starting to sound irritated, obviously wishing he'd go elsewhere with his questions. "It just happens here."

"Why?"

"I'm not a psychiatrist. I've got enough trouble trying to keep peoples' bodies intact without worrying about their heads. I can't tell you why. I suppose some people just can't take it here after a while." She grinned humorlessly. "Can't imagine why not. Io in the Spring is such a lovely place. If you want a preview of Hell. Never thought you'd be offered a chance to work there. I always thought Hell was a permanent sign-up."

"The two suicides. Did you do autopsies?"

"No."

"Why not?"

She finally stopped and turned to face him, gave him a disbelieving glance. When she saw that he was serious, she explained, speaking slowly and carefully as if to a child.

"In the first place, the Company wanted the bodies shipped out quickly. They don't tell me why. I guess because they feel that having the corpses of a lot of suicided folks hanging around might be bad for morale.

"Secondly, when somebody exposes themselves to near zero-pressure atmosphere there isn't a lot to inspect. You can't run an autopsy through a food processor. And in the third place, you're becoming a nuisance."

O'Niel reached out and yanked open a drawer, blocking her intended path.

"I know. It's a bad habit."

She sighed, looked boredly up at him, and waited for him to finish.

"I would like," he continued pleasantly, "a record of all incidents like these last two that have happened during the past six months. I would like it real soon, or I just might kick your nasty ass all over this room." He smiled thinly, pushed the drawer back in. "That's a Marshal joke."

He spun on his heel and marched out of the hospital. She watched him leave, then turned back to her work.

Sagan was looking forward to the night. His shift had gone well: no glitches, no problems, no arguments. No breakdowns requiring anything more than the usual amount of sweat.

Even the foreman had managed an occasional kind word, and his assistant LaVille had finally conquered his damnable cold to the point where he no longer shattered everyone's eardrums by sneezing through the suit coms.

The exchange in the locker room had gone

smoothly, as always. Around him in the lavatory his co-workers were likewise preparing themselves to go off duty or on, as their shift schedules dictated.

He finished smoothing the depilatory cream on his face, waited a moment before wiping it and whiskers off with a clean towel. He followed this treatment by applying an aftershave with a heavy aroma and erotic name.

The final result he admired in the mirror. Not bad, he told himself. He joked with a passing friend on the way to the showers, exchanged comments on the day's work with another, then strolled back to the bunkroom. He wore only undershorts.

The aisles were relatively deserted, though the dormitory was never what could be called dead silent. Dim sounds from the video players at the far end of the aisle reached him, while the noise of individual viewers whispered faintly from open or sealed bunks.

Sagan's private little world was on Level Two of Aisle Seven. Its location was a reflection of his comparatively short tenure at the mine.

The most experienced workers, those who'd been longest on Io, occupied the topmost bunks of Level Four, which were the quietest and offered the greatest amount of privacy. A man on Level Four could lie in bed and gaze upward in the knowledge that no one else was tossing and turning above him. This system was not instituted by the Company but by the workers themselves, though it was as thoroughly enforced as any of the more formal regulations.

The multiple tour men, the Jove-jockies, had

the bunks in the corners near the back of the dormitory. These were away from the video screens and much of the noise from the bathroom. They were almost peaceful.

Sagan often envied the old-timers their nearly private quarters, but he had no intention of sticking around long enough to qualify for one. The moment his single-year tour was up, he'd cash in his bonus and head home.

That was still in the future. For now there was tonight.

He climbed into his bunk with the ease of practice, flipped on his reading lamp. At a touch the privacy screens slid shut. He reached into one of the drawers set into the foot of the bed and fumbled under the clothing inside.

The vaccination gun he withdrew was compact, a blunt gun-shape that was mostly nozzle and trigger. The gun was not illegal. Most of the workers had authorizations permitting their ownership. It made the distribution of medicines much simpler when the dispensary could ship capsules to each worker's bunk instead of having to call them into the hospital one at a time. Such trips wasted work time.

The tiny half-transparent vial that Sagan excavated from behind the drawer was smaller than his thumbnail. He slid back the breech and slipped the vial into the gun's receiving chamber. A quick check showed that the gun's air cylinder was appropriately charged.

Pressing the nozzle hard against his inner thigh, he pulled the trigger. A burst of air forced the vial's contents into his leg.

He leaned back and inhaled deeply, closing

his eyes. After a few minutes he returned the gun to its drawer and slid the compartment shut.

Opening another compartment he selected a shirt. Whistling blithely, he began to get dressed.

It was night in O'Niel's quarters. It was also quiet. He liked the night, a familiar old friend who never surprised him no matter where he was stationed. The quiet was different, a reflection of the hole in his heart.

He was sitting on the couch, which obediently gave support in the right places to his slightly softening frame. I'm a lot like the couch, he thought. Tough framework, flexible, fully capable of handling several people simultaneously, yet getting soft around the middle.

The analogy was not unique. O'Niel was a man used to regarding people as furniture, objects that occupied space in rooms and chambers.

He considered some of his newer acquaintances, diverting his mind from other, less pleasant thoughts in the silent room to an old mental game.

Montone, his first Sergeant: now there was a man a lot like a newly refurbished chair. Bright and shiny, very efficient looking, yet untested. Paint could hide a lot. Eventually he'd have to dig a little or he'd never know just how dependable Montone was.

Sheppard ... Sheppard reminded him of a big desk. One that looked like sturdy old oak. Solid and immovable, ready to take whatever was dumped on it. Only he suspected that a lot of Sheppard was veneer. Strip that away and you were likely to find not oak underneath, but wood pulp held together with glue. Cheap.

Dr. Lazarus . . . now there was a real antique, and no veneer. Beaten up, a little worm-eaten, unattractive on the outside, but well-made. Maybe. Furniture like that was hard to figure from a single look. It might hold a horse, might collapse under the slightest real pressure. And the nails stuck out of the woodwork at odd angles. If you weren't careful, you might get jabbed.

A knock sounded at the door. He shifted his feet on the small, shiny coffee table and tried to rouse himself from his self-imposed lethargy, with little success.

Hell with it, he thought disconsolately. There was no one in the apartment to be polite for.

"It's open."

Montone entered, carrying a large tray filled with covered plates. He set the tray down on the coffee table, forcing O'Niel to move his feet.

"I don't know what you like to eat, so I brought a little of everything. Some of it actually tastes different from the rest."

O'Niel looked at the food containers and tried to smile thankfully at the sergeant. The expression that resulted was not as encouraging as he'd intended.

Montone sounded honestly concerned as he sat down in the chair across from O'Niel.

"Listen, you have to eat something. If nothing else, it helps kill the monotony. I'm an expert on that. Always got ribbed about my name. Mind if I join you? Thanks," he finished before O'Niel had a chance to reply.

Montone rose, walked into the kitchenette area and hunted through the cabinets until he found a glass which might have seemed like an unwarranted luxury to a stranger. It wasn't.

A couple of the first engineers sent to build the mine had spent their spare time working up a small, automated glass-making facility. Io had plenty of raw material. The glass was one of the few items of household use that was produced locally.

Returning, Montone sat down opposite O'Niel again and started taking the covers off the food.

"There's chocolate cake for dessert, except you can't have any until you finish all your meat."

O'Niel smiled in spite of himself. He knew that Montone was on his own off-time. He didn't have to be here.

"I know how you feel," the sergeant was telling him sincerely. "I do."

O'Niel just stared at him.

"Think I'm just saying that?" He leaned forward, picked at the food as he spoke. "The second time I did a tour, I came home and found that my wife had skipped off with some guy who's a computer programmer. Little fishy-looking twit who's losing his hair." O'Niel studied him.

"I have two daughters," Montone went on, chewing a piece of real steak. "They call the programmer 'daddy.' My wife said she was happy. The guy looks so boring! She said he may not be Mr. Excitement, but he was home all the time." He hesitated, looked down toward the floor.

"Can't argue with that." He pushed the big tray toward O'Niel. "Try the food...it's not that bad. The Admin kitchen here is pretty good. A lot better than some I've tried. Sometimes they even get real meat." He gestured at the plates. "Sheppard busts his butt to get the top people the best. You can say that for him." If he was waiting for a reaction from O'Niel he was disappointed.

"The steak's real. Give it a shot."

"I will."

Montone continued to speak without meeting O'Niel's eyes. "You know, the hookers here are nice. Io's got a tough rep for duty but a good one for off-time. Sometimes when you're lonely, they can help. Most of them are good at what they do, and they're all Company okay'd."

"I'm sure."

There was a period of quiet while Montone nibbled at his portion. After a while he looked up.

"You want to play cards?" He grinned. "I cheat. Except I cheat so badly you can catch me."

"No, thank you."

Montone looked disappointed. "I get the feeling I'm bombing."

"No." O'Niel tried to sound grateful. "I really appreciate what you're doing. I really do. It's just...it's just that I would like to be alone right now."

Montone rose from the chair. "I understand, Marshal." He started for the door. "I'll handle the next shift reports and make up the duty roster. You want to check it? I can put a copy through your monitor." He gestured toward the computer console in the corner. O'Niel simply shook his head.

"Not necessary, Sargeant."

"All right. If you need anything. If you just want to talk ... please call me." He smiled. "My rates are pretty reasonable."

"Thank you. I mean it."

"Screw it." He nodded toward the still steaming tray of food. "You can have the chocolate cake. I'm on a diet." He closed the door quietly as he left.

O'Niel was smiling as his subordinate departed. The smile was for the benefit of a concerned friend, however, and was less than genuine. It faded rapidly once Montone was gone.

His gaze traveled down to the table and the food waiting there. Montone had gone out of his way to make the meal sound appetizing, but O'Niel didn't want to touch it.

Like a wind-up toy he stood, moved to the console, switched on one of the monitors, and entered a command.

O'NIEL, W.T. PLAYBACK WEDNESDAY TRANSMISSIONS

The screen flickered. The message request vanished to be replaced by the mechanical reply.

O'NIEL, W.T. AFFIRMATIVE. REPLAY WEDNESDAY TRANSMISSIONS ....

An image solidified on the screen, became Montone.

"Marshal, we got a response on your request . . . ."

O'Niel touched another control. The picture speeded into comedy, the sound turning to high-pitched gibberish. The squeaky wail slowed as a tone sounded and O'Niel's finger moved across another control.

A new face appeared. "Marshal," the portrait said, "it's Caldwell in West Security. We got a small problem here, nothing serious, but I just wanted to get your opinion on it before we proc . . . ."

Again the previous stud cut off the chatter in midsentence, again the recording fast-forwarded to finish with a signaling tone. Down went the second control.

Carol's face appeared. "I . . . I'm trying to keep my composure and . . . and like everything else I do . . . I think I'm messing this up."

O'Niel sat down in the chair and stared fixedly at the screen, as attentive as though he were seeing it for the first time.

"I despise these message things," Carol was saying, the words bouncing around inside O'Niel's skull. "I . . . I'm just such a coward. I couldn't stand there in person face to face with you and say what I'm about to say. I just couldn't.

"If you were in front of me right now, I would change my mind. And I don't want to change my mind."

A yellow light winked above the screen, accompanied by a high-pitched beep. O'Niel picked up the closed-channel audio receiver nearby, automatically activating it. His eyes never left the monitor.

"O'Niel here." He listened. "What? How bad?" At the other end of the thin glass thread a voice was talking too fast. "I'll be right there."

He let the receiver slip back into its socket, moving rapidly now. Near the door a small riot gun hung in a loop support. It looked a lot like an old sawed-off shotgun save for much smoother lines and some complex instrumentation. Automatically he checked the velocity setting, made sure it read INDOOR — CLOSE QUARTERS, then opened the door and rushed out of the apartment.

Behind him the video screen, left unattended, continued to spill its recorded trauma.

"I love you. Please know that." Pause. "Look at me. I'm asking for your approval."

The voice rambled on, alternately crying and declaiming, pleading to an empty room . . . .

V

O'Niel rushed through the corridors, down swaying accessway tubes. Workers and administrators got out of his way without having to be asked. They watched his retreating back and conversed in low tones until he was long gone. None of them had the slightest idea what was going on, but they all knew no security personnel ran like that without a damned good reason. And there was the riot gun held firmly in the Marshal's hands.

At the end of the corridor mentioned in the call O'Niel found a pair of deputies waiting for him. He couldn't give them names, but that didn't matter right now.

"He's in the West Wing, Marshal," the woman informed him. She looked worried, angry, and a little frightened. Not for herself—for someone else. If she were frightened for herself she didn't show it.

O'Niel nodded a cursory thank you and entered the passageway beyond the checkpoint. Behind him the two deputies kept the curious turned away.

Further on he found Montone and another deputy, both carrying weapons similar to O'Niel's. They held them tightly and not with the easy grip favored during routine patrol.

Montone nodded down the corridor. It was lined with closed doors. At the far end was the central Club. Faint music from it drifted up the corridor.

"He's in a leisure compartment," the sergeant explained in a low, tight tone. "He's with a hooker. All we know is that the guy is roughing her up. She pushed the alarm."

"Who answered?"

The deputy replied. "When I responded to the alarm and tried the door, the man told me he had a knife. He said he'd kill her if I didn't leave immediately." Her expression never changed. "There's no video inside. Privacy circuit's engaged. But I didn't have to see it to know he has it. All you have to do is listen to his voice. So I backed off."

O'Niel nodded approvingly. "Who is he? Were you able to find out?"

She nodded again. "He was seen going in and the girl registered him on entrance, as per procedure, recorded his marker to her account, and had it verified for a plus balance. He's a crane operator. Been here almost eleven months, Personnel says."

"Eleven . . . hell," Montone muttered.

"Never caused any trouble," the deputy continued. "No record of any kind, no previous mention of anything like this. I checked for instability, perversion . . . the usual. He's clean. His shiftmates like him. At least, those I could contact said they did. Foreman said he's a good worker, gives a hundred percent when he's on the job. Name is Sagan. When I told them what was going on, none of 'em believed me."

"How's the girl?"

It was Montone's turn to comment. "She's still alive. You can hear her moaning over the com. Beyond that . . . ." He shrugged meaningfully.

They turned, walked down the corridor and halted before the specified door. Four more armed deputies awaited them there, milling around and whispering urgently. They shut up and made room for O'Niel and the sergeant.

"Is he stoned?" O'Niel asked, examining the door.

"Beats me." Montone's lips worked. "Some guys just like to slap hookers around. But this is more."

O'Niel looked back at the deputy who'd first reacted to the alarm. "You sure he's got a knife?"

"There's no port and the privacy circuit's locked in. These gals like their privacy and so do their tricks. There's no way to be sure he hasn't got one. I'd bet that he does."

"Why? Because of the way he sounds?"

"Not just that," she told him quietly. "Because of the way the girl sounds."

O'Niel nodded once, as if that was proof

enough. He turned and pounded forcefully on the door, speaking into the transceiver set in the metal.

"Sagan!" he shouted. "This is Marshal O'Niel. Let the girl go and no one is going to hurt you. We just want to help you." There was no response from the other side. "Can you hear me, Sagan?"

The room was small, painted in warm, cloying tones, and held two pieces of furniture: a video monitor and a bed. A film of a type not suitable for family viewing was unspooling on the monitor. Neither of the room's occupants was paying it any attention.

Sagan lay on his back on the bed, naked from the waist up. Perspiration flowed off his body, soaking the sheets beneath him.

There was much too much sweat, too much for a man who'd undergone hours of strenuous exercise, which Sagan had not. It beaded up on his lips and forehead, poured freely from under his arms. His eyes were wild and his expression demonic. He was smiling, a chilling grin as frozen as the outside of the mine.

One arm was tight around the chest of a young, brunette girl, who generally looked older than she was. Fear had wiped the experience off her face now. She looked as young as she was. She was slim and quite naked. The sheets under her were in disarray.

With his other hand Sagan held the knife which was long and thin and gleamed brightly in the room's subdued light. The point just puckered the skin of the girl's throat, barely indenting the pale flesh, forcing her head back at a painful, unnatural angle.

She was bleeding, not from the throat but from a broken nose and split lower lip. Her jaw was turning purple and starting to swell from some terrible blow. Barely conscious, which was a blessing, she bubbled a steady whimper from her throat, from behind the knife.

"Get away from me!" Sagan yelled at the door. "I'll kill her . . . I swear to God I will. I'll slit her throat. It won't take me very long, you know. I can do it real fast if you make me."

"Why?" O'Niel's voice came coaxingly out of the speaker set in the door. "What has she done?"

"She's evil." Sagan was breathing hard and fast, like a man who couldn't get his breath. Plenty of fresh air circulated through the room but his throat was constricted.

"I want you to go away. Now! I will slice her little pink throat right this minute if you don't go away! I will slice it right through."

He pushed a little harder on the knife handle. The point barely broke the skin. A tiny red dot appeared, grew into a globule and broke to trickle viscously down the side of the girl's neck.

She was not so dazed that she couldn't scream in terror but she had sense enough left not to fight.

"Hey!" O'Niel yelled quickly as the scream echoed out into the corridor. "Listen to me. Just listen. I can't go away, and you know that. Now, nobody's going to hurt you. I want you to understand that, Sagan. If you want to talk, we'll talk. I won't try to break in. Does that sound fair? I don't break in and you don't do anything crazy with the girl, okay?"

Silence from inside. "Sagan, do you hear me?"

A response came from the transceiver . . . of a sort, a series of bleating noises, part whine, part growl, very much more animal than human.

O'Niel glanced to one side and motioned at one of the armed deputies. The man hurried over.

"Get me a maintenance worker," O'Niel ordered. "One who's familiar with this section. And fast." He jerked a hand toward the door. "The guy's on the edge and going over, understand?"

The wide-eyed deputy nodded vigorously and raced for the communications box located at the far end of the corridor.

"Hey, Sagan. Sagan, it's me again, the Marshal." O'Niel forced himself to keep his voice even and seemingly unconcerned. No pleading, no false sympathy. Someone in Sagan's mental condition was more likely to react dangerously to that than to a direct threat.

"Sagan . . . try to understand what I'm saying. Take a minute and think. You haven't gone too far yet. You follow me? All they can get you for so far is a little roughhousing. As long as you don't kill the girl, everything can work out.

"Think about it, man. You've got less than a month left on your tour. You've got completion time bonus money coming. You're almost on your way home. Don't mess it up now."

On the other side of the door, Sagan was giggling. Not at O'Niel, not at the girl, not at himself, but at something inside his head even he couldn't see clearly.

"I'm going to cut this pretty little thing up. I'm going to use my nice shiny clean knife and I'm going to do it slowly. Soooo slooowww-ly . . . ."

Choking sounds, tiny and weak, were audible beneath that softly chuckled pronouncement. O'Niel considered. Sagan sounded very determined.

A maintenance woman came running up the corridor toward him, the deputy who'd called her pacing alongside. Her coveralls were full of tools and her equipment belt jiggled. She was gasping for breath as she halted next to O'Niel.

He had no time to let her relax. "Show me which panel leads to the flow duct for this compartment."

She nodded at him, took out a long tool, and moved to the left of the door. The tool moved four times and four bolts fell from a metal square set high in the corridor wall. The square was equidistant between the door to Sagan's cave and the one on its left.

The worker slipped the tool back into her belt, grabbed the panel with both hands and jerked. It came away, revealing a narrow crawlway leading into darkness.

"When I give the word I want you to close the hydraulic valve that operates the door lock," he told her. "That'll spring it."

She set the panel down as she listened to him, then moved to stand ready next to a smaller square. She flipped it open. Lights and glowing readouts showed inside.

While O'Niel mentioned hydraulics to the worker, Montone was already speaking to a pair of deputies. They followed him into the waiting, open ductway and began moving inward, making as little noise as possible.

O'Niel waited until the last deputy had disappeared down the narrow passage, then walked back to the door. He made a cautionary gesture to the young maintenance engineer standing ready next to the open control panel. She nodded solemnly, her hand positioned over the appropriate switch.

O'Niel made sure the riot gun was ready, leaned close to the door as he addressed the transceiver once more. "Sagan! Can you hear me?"

At the sound of O'Niel's voice the man inside abruptly rose from the bed and began pacing the room, searching corners and walls. The girl watched him. She was breathing a little easier now that the knife had left her throat where blood still trickled lazily down her neck. She didn't try to run: there was no place to run to. She just sat there, watching him, her jaw throbbing agonizingly, and strove not to twitch.

Sagan turned circles, silently screaming at the walls. He no longer looked human.

"I hear you!" he shouted hysterically. "Of course I can hear you! Do you think I'm deaf?"

"No, no, of course I don't think you're deaf," O'Niel told him soothingly. "I just wanted to make sure you were hearing me, is all.

"I'm going to explain something to you now, Sagan. I'm going to explain it very carefully, and I'd be grateful if you'd pay attention."

Sagan hunted for the voice, flailing and slashing at the air with his knife. The voice was all around him and it threatened to drown out the other voice, the one inside his head that made such naughty suggestions and promised such delicious, nasty pleasures.

The light Montone used was small, intentionally so, as he edged his way along the metal tunnel, bumping his head and skinning his hands, hardly daring to breathe lest the sound leak into the room they were paralleling. He could hear the panting of the two men crawling behind him.

"I can't let you stay in there forever," O'Niel's voice was telling Sagan with maddening self-assurance. The words echoed around the room and the crane operator chopped at it with his blade. "You'll hurt yourself."

A scratching noise reached O'Niel. He looked curiously at the transceiver, wondering for an instant if it had malfunctioned.

Then he realized what it was: Sagan was using the knife on the speaker, trying to cut it off, trying to cut out the patient sound of the Marshal's voice. A moan came through the transceiver over the scraping. This time it was a man's voice.

"I'm going to release the hydraulic pressure on the door locks," he told Sagan slowly. "It will cause the door to swing open, in spite of anything you can do." He looked away from the pickup, at the tall deputy who was peering down the flow duct. The deputy had been marking the progress of Montone and the others. Now he flashed O'Niel a pre-arranged sign.

The Marshal turned back to the pickup. "You can't keep the door closed, Sagan. The moment the hydraulics are cut off it will open inward.

You can't stay in there. You might as well come out.

"Be sensible, Sagan. You're still safe, still in the clear. Why don't you just walk out and make it easy on yourself?"

Sagan's voice rose in response, came harshly through the speaker and rattled around the silent corridor. "The second that door opens, I'm going to kill her! I'm going to slice her. I hate her!"

Montone hesitated, looked to his right. There were four small hinges set against the inner wall of the crawlway. According to the maintenance engineer they held the panel which opened into the sealed compartment.

Holding the small flashlight in his mouth, he started feeling for the hinges. Gingerly, he tugged one inward—it slid open silently and efficiently. There was no warning snap. Quickly he started working on the second hinge. He could hear Sagan raving on the other side of the wall.

O'Niel spoke while checking his chronometer. He couldn't wait for Montone much longer, not judging from the sound of the crane operator's voice.

"I'm not going to argue with you, Sagan, and I'm not going to try and trick you. I am going to count down from ten to one. At one, the door will open slowly. I will not rush in. I'm not going to do anything that will alarm you, and I'm not going to shoot you.

"I don't want anybody hurt, including you. It's my job to see that people *don't* get hurt, not the other way 'round. I don't think you really want to hurt anybody either, Sagan. Not really." He watched the seconds tick away on the chronometer.

"Please trust me. Whatever the problem is, whatever's making you do this, we can work it out without anyone having to get hurt. I promise. It'll be better that way, both for you and for me."

Montone felt the last hinge give way, leaving the panel balancing loosely in its slot. It was hard not to fight for air in that cramped passageway but he forced himself to breathe in slow, open-mouthed gasps. He was ready. A check showed the same was true of the two men who'd accompanied him. They were waiting for a cue from O'Niel.

Sagan had finally stopped stumbling about the room. The knife dangled from his limp right hand and the wild fire in his eyes had turned to a faintly glazed look. O'Niel's calming words were beginning to have an effect.

"You're . . . you're going to kill me," Sagan murmured uncertainly toward the door. For the first time, he sounded confused instead of fanatically confident.

"I'm not," O'Niel rushed to assure him. He allowed himself to feel some hope. "You have my word. You also have my word that if you kill the girl, I *will* kill you." He turned, lifted his hand as a signal to the maintenance engineer, then spoke once more into the pickup.

"Now listen carefully, Sagan. I'm going to do what I told you a moment ago. I'm going to count slowly from ten to one. Just do as I say and everything will work out all right. Ten, nine . . . ."

Sagan stood swaying in the compartment,

fighting to reason his way through the ugly nimbus of hate which had taken control of his thoughts. His expression had turned blank, his brain overloaded by too much contradictory information. Only moments earlier everything had seemed so straightforward, so simple. Now . . . .

O'Niel's voice reached him from somewhere far away. "Eight, seven . . ."

In the crawlway Montone's right hand tightened on the hatch, preparatory to flinging it aside. He could hear O'Niel's voice from the speaker inside the compartment.

"Six . . . five . . . four . . ." The maintenance engineer's finger caressed the cutoff switch.

" . . . three . . . two . . ."

Sagan turned a slow half circle, stood gazing dumbly at the doorway. There was a soft clang from behind him as the panel covering the flow duct access sprang in and upward on springs to slap against the wall. Montone dropped into the room as Sagan whirled to see what had caused the noise. O'Niel's voice still echoed in his ears.

" . . . one . . . ."

Montone fired. The explosion of the riot gun was stunning in the small compartment. The girl came fully out of her self-enforced paralysis with a scream that rose above the roar of the gun.

At the same time the engineer thumbed the switch. There was a quick, almost inaudible rushing sound from inside the door as it slid inward.

O'Niel stood there, staring through the open

doorway, his own gun held loosely in both hands: he'd heard the explosion. Quickly he scanned the interior of the compartment, taking stock, summing up.

The girl was okay. She lay on the bed, crying softly to herself and holding her arms tightly across her chest. He noted the blood dribbling down her neck onto her chest, and hoped that the wound wasn't serious.

His attention shifted leftward to where Sagan lay on the floor, arms and legs spraddled and his head cocked at an angle much too acute. There was a gaping, smoking hole where his chest should have been. His eyes were locked open, staring vacantly toward the ceiling.

Montone looked at the Marshal, his mouth working weakly. "He turned on me. I . . . I saw the knife . . . ."

O'Niel continued to stare silently, unable to believe the scene in the room. He shook his head and gazed in disbelief at Montone.

The two deputies who'd accompanied the sergeant had dropped into the compartment and were busy administering first aid to the girl, while others clustered behind O'Niel, straining for a look inward. They gaped at the remains of the crane operator, at the girl, at Montone, and muttered to themselves.

You don't move slowly on a place like Io and save others. The two paramedics fairly burst through the emergency entrance of the hospital, convoying the gurney between them. On it lay the unconscious, shocked body of the unlucky young prostitute. A tube ran from a bot-

tle held by one of the paramedics into her arm.
Deputies led the way with O'Niel two steps
behind.

Dr. Lazarus was waiting for them at the
emergency entrance and was examining the
girl, taking readings and making measure-
ments, as they rushed her to intensive care.

There was commotion without confusion.
Everyone knew his job. They were spurred to
still faster action by Lazarus' stream of orders.
The duty nurse was trying to organize everything and not succeeding as well as she would
have liked.

Inside the emergency area Lazarus and the
paramedics stripped the protective sterilizing
sheet from the girl's body, then slid her, gurney
and all, into a long, glassine tube. Lazarus
moved to the computer console built into the
side of the tube and began punching out directions.

A low hum rose from somewhere beneath the
cylinder that started to rotate. Instantly three
nearby video screens came awake with a pleth-
ora of information. Two displayed diagrammat-
ics of the girl's body, giving reports on everything from skeletal stability to circulatory flow.
The third screen was awash with numbers and
words delineating blood pressure, temperature,
white cell count, and so on.

O'Niel waited nearby, studying the girl,
watching the information change on the monitors, and wished he knew more than minimal
medicine. Devoid of its usual coolness, her
bruised face looked almost innocent.

It was worse than he'd guessed at first
glance.

"Jaw looks broken," Lazarus was mumbling. "At least in one place, maybe more. Possibly the nose as well. Contusions all over the body and face. Neck wound is superficial, thank God." She spared time to throw O'Niel a disbelieving glance.

"Jesus Christ, who did this to her?"

"A worker." His attention was still on the girl. "Crane operator, supposedly stable as they come. He went nuts. It happens here . . . remember?"

She gave him a look but spared the sarcasm that instinctively welled up in her. Maybe she deserved the dig. She'd been something less than cordial to O'Niel during their first meeting.

In any case, this wasn't the time and place for verbal sparring.

"No skull fractures," she announced, carefully examining the blowup of one diagram. "By the way, I got that list you wanted. She's bleeding internally downstairs. Damn the man, whoever he is and whatever was wrong with him. I'd like to get him in here."

"You won't. He's dead."

Lazarus' quick reaction was understandable, if unhippocratic. "Good."

"Why didn't you bring it to my office?" O'Niel asked her.

"The list?" She adjusted a control. Inside the cylinder a small nozzle pressed against the girl's bruised belly, then withdrew. It didn't appear to have done anything, but numbers changed rapidly on the third monitor and the girl shifted slightly. "I don't make house calls."

"You do now." He looked a last time at the girl. "She going to be all right?"

"Maybe . . . if you let me do my job."

O'Niel smiled, nodded briefly and moved away.

Off to the right was a section of white wall lined with large drawers resembling a hive. It served as the mine's morgue. The transparent faces of each drawer were fogged with cold. Lazarus continued working behind him, her sole attention on the girl in the cylinder.

O'Niel studied the drawers. The fog didn't completely obliterate the interiors and bodies would be visible within. After several minutes of careful inspection a frown broke out on his face. The two examining tables arranged in front of the drawers were unoccupied. A closer look gave no sign that they'd been in recent use.

A voice sounded from immediately behind him. "Twenty-eight, in six months."

He turned, saw Lazarus standing nearby. She looked worn, but then she always looked worn.

"I wonder how many in the six months before that?" he murmured interestedly.

"Twenty-four. I've got initiative."

"Good for you."

He turned back to the wall and began pulling out the body drawers. They were clean, antisepticized, and empty.

Lazarus watched him. "You want to know how many in the six months before that? Hmmm? Go on, ask me how many in the six months before that."

He turned to her, asked the question with his eyes.

"Two," she told him.

"Two." He stared down at her. "You notice anything?"

"I'm unpleasant," she replied, "but I'm not stupid. Of course I notice something. Funny numbers, and they don't come from the gaming machines in the Club."

"What do you think?"

"I don't know what to think." She sounded confused as well as exhausted. "Almost everybody here doesn't have both oars in the water as far as I'm concerned. Why people suddenly start to lose their marbles in greater numbers is not so mystifying to me. I don't know why more of them haven't done it sooner."

O'Niel pulled out the last drawer. It was as vacant as the others, the sheets unstained, the air inside fragrant with ammonia and other disinfectants. He shut the drawer with a vicious push.

The morgue's lack of occupants raised several interesting questions, foremost among them being the fact that Sagan's body wasn't anywhere to be found. He could think of excuses for the other empty drawers, but the crane operator ought to be resting quietly in one of them.

"Where do they send the bodies?"

"They usually put them on the first shuttle out. They wrap them up and jettison the body halfway to the support station. Burial at sea and all that crap." Lazarus was not a closet

romantic. Io welcomed realists, dealt harshly
with displaced dreamers.

"The Company tries to pass it off as glamor-
ous and proper. You know, 'we now commend
his body to the vast reaches of the frontier he
helped to push back a little farther.' What
they're doing is saving freight charges back to
Earth, or wherever home was. It's efficient. It
sucks, but it's efficient."

Very efficient, O'Niel had to agree.

The freight dock was deserted. It was the
largest pressurized structure on Io. When the
shuttle docked the cavernous chamber was a
sea of activity with men and machines swarm-
ing around the shuttle in an attempt to complete their tasks in the shortest possible time.
Huge hopper cars were raised and their pre-
processed ore dumped into the shuttle's cargo
bays. Containers and people flowed out of the
bulky vessel.

There was no shuttle sealed to the dock now.
The next ore load wasn't due from the mine 'til
the end of the night shift. Relays snapped and
clicked as machinery hummed in man's absence, performing maintenance and checking
functions that had once required human super-
vision.

Everything functioned smoothly. The dock
waited in silence for the next scheduled burst
of activity.

High-intensity funnel lights hung from long
tubes keeping portions of the dock illuminated.
At the far end of the chamber was the huge
airlock which would open to envelop the arriving shuttle. It was well lit. Much of the rest

of the dock and its mountains of containers and ore carriers lay in darkness.

Something flitted from one shadow to the next, dodging cautiously around the bright pools of light that fell from above. It was small compared to the .massive ore carriers. There was no one around to notice the movement.

From time to time the figure would pause to check the sealed bills of lading heat-stamped into each outgoing container. The larger ones the figure ignored. It was the non-ore carriers that occupied its interest. Every container had the Con-Amalgamated company logo stamped prominently on sides and top.

O'Niel moved stealthily from one container to the next, always checking to make sure he was alone. He'd worked his way across the length of the dock before he came across two containers near the airlock transship loader which bore stamps of interest.

His gaze traveled over the nearest, noting the bill of lading and list of contents, the word "fragile" stamped below the manifest. After careful perusal of the inventory he moved on to inspect the second container. Instead of fragile it carried the imprinted instructions, "To Be Jettisoned" on one side.

A last cautionary glance revealed nothing moving in the vast docking chamber. O'Niel's breathing seemed unnaturally loud to him as he methodically unsnapped the four latches which sealed the container's north end. Each let free with a booming metallic click as it was released. O'Niel caught his breath at each snap, but no one arrived to investigate.

Using both hands and getting his weight behind the effort he heaved the sliding panel to the right. He snapped on his flashlight and began probing the container's interior.

The beam danced over long stacks of metal boxes, sealed cylinders, plastic cubes, and heat-sealed lumps of garbage. Each bore the ancient triple red triangle that warned of the presence of radioactive waste. The mine and its complex equipment was wholly solar-powered, but many individual sections like the hospital used radioactive components, as did certain pieces of equipment.

Buried near the lower left side of the container was a silver mylar sack. Full of lumps, it seemed out of place alongside the sleek disposable radiation packs.

O'Niel checked the warning patch sewn into the right sleeve of his jacket. It was still bright green and showed no tendency toward turning yellow or worse, orange. Io's radioactive wastes were strictly low-grade. He could safely carry out his little inspection

The bag was sealed with a plastic zipper. He broke the snap-seal and pulled the tab down. Hair appeared first. It was quickly followed by a forehead, then a nose flanked by a pair of eyes still frozen open.

O'Niel didn't linger on the silent, accusing face. The heavy zipper was dragged down until the red-stained padding that covered the hole in Sagan's chest was exposed. O'Niel fumbled at his breast pocket. For an instant he thought he'd lost it. Then his fingers closed around the shaft of the power syringe.

He paused, wiped a forearm across his eyes, and took a couple of deep breaths. Then he positioned the syringe precisely over the artery at the base of the dead man's neck. The liquid inside the corpse no longer flowed; the internal pump had been stilled. But the power draw in the syringe pulled a thick blue-red fluid up into the tube.

For once he had reason to be grateful for the Company's penurious policies. Since the body was about to be consigned forever to the limitless graveyard of space, there was no need for embalming. What the syringe sucked out of poor Sagan's system was still a part of him . . . .

VI

The beeping wouldn't go away.

Ever since she was a little girl she'd been tormented by nightmares and their sounds. You'll outgrow them, she'd been told by fatuous adults and doctors. They're only figments of your imagination, sent by the boogeyman to bedevil your girlish dreams.

Bullshit.

If anything, there was a period of adulthood when her somnolent imaginings had been more terrifying than anything she'd conjured up as a child. That had finally faded away.

Now the occasional bad dream was simply a familiar and unwelcome visitor, to be tolerated for a little while and then sent on its way. Like an in-law, she mused.

It was a funny thing, though. During her first tour she'd discovered that sleeping off-Earth lessened the frequency of her nightmares, kept them almost at bay. Once again, doctors' explanations proved useless.

She didn't much care. The further out from Earth she traveled, the rarer her nightmares came a-visiting. It was a phenomenon other travelers had remarked on, and it was driving the psychiatrists crazy. Fair enough, she thought.

Io was about as far out as you could get, unless you were part of the deep-probe team still coasting toward far Neptune, or with the present team that was preparing Titan for exploitation. She was way past being probe material, or even preset. No, Io was as far out as she'd ever get. If it weren't for the peacefulness granted by the absence of the nightmares, she'd have returned to the warm Earth long ago.

It's all in your mind, her psych friends had assured her. You've cured yourself. If you go home you'll be safe from bad dreams. You'll see.

All in her mind? She'd heard that one before, as a child. Anyway, there were other reasons for remaining Outland. For one thing, she had no home to go back to. No relatives, no roots. Not anymore. Not for some time.

Now she lived within the narrow diameter of test vial and microscope, which were room enough to house her remaining aspirations. Her only other real concern was simply to continue To Get Through the Night.

She tossed on the bed. It had been months

since anything this strong had troubled her. The beeping continued relentlessly, vibrating inside her skull. There was no imagery associated with it. Peculiar . . . a purely aural nightmare. An intriguing thought: perhaps it wasn't a nightmare at all.

She opened her eyes, blinked at the darkness. The beeping continued.

Too tired to curse, she rolled over and acknowledged the com call. The voice at the other end was deep, persistent, vaguely familiar. She tried to make some sense out of it, mumbling groggily, "Hello?"

"Lazarus, this is O'Niel," the voice announced tersely. "I'll see you in the hospital right away."

She struggled to a sitting position. Fumbling fingers found the reading light suspended over the bed. The hospital lit up and she pushed aside the sheets covering the examination table she'd been sleeping on.

A glance at the luminescent wall chronometer did nothing to improve her temper. "Do you know what time it is?"

"Yes."

"You better be dying." She hung up.

It was better than a real nightmare, but not much. Waking had its own terror. She set the com receiver back in its slot and slid her legs over the side of the table. By the light of the reading lamp she staggered over to the nearest basin, threw cold water on her face and roughly toweled it dry. Makeup she didn't bother with, having given up on that long ago in favor of more subtle maskery.

True to his words, the Marshal arrived moments later. In one hand he held a syringe which Lazarus' practised eye immediately noted was full of something organic. He held it out to her, breathing hard.

"Very pretty," she commented drily, studying the proferred cylinder.

"So are you. I need this analyzed."

"You woke me at this hour for a goddamn analysis?" She was too upset to be really angry.

"It's important." Something in his voice told her that he was probably understating.

Even so, she growled at him. "It'd better be."

She led him over to a console, studied it a moment and then touched several controls. Small video screens came to life, a rack with four tubes held in tiny metal fingers popped out of the wall.

Measuring quickly but precisely she split the contents of the syringe between the four tubes, then touched another control. The rack slid back into the wall. The laboratory area remained dark, the only light coming from the powered-up screens and keyboard and the distant reading light burning above the examination table.

O'Niel searched cold twilight, found a chair, and pulled it close to the console.

"How long will this take?"

"You're kidding me. This is a hospital, not a security depot. When we ask questions, that means we need answers fast." She pointed to the screens, where rows of information were already beginning to materialize.

O'Niel indicated the first column. "What does that mean?"

"Nothing much." She squinted in the dim light, studying the readout. "Blood type, cholesterol count, white cell count, oxygenation ... this blood is from a dead person. Or else somebody beyond my help."

"Right the first time."

She smiled thinly. "The symptoms are pretty plain. Unfortunately, the condition's not curable." More information appeared, forming glowing lines on the screens.

"No alcohol," she muttered. There was another run of data as the analyzer continued its methodical breakdown of the liquid O'Niel had fed it.

"He ate dinner," she soon announced. "Proteins, carbohydrates ... more carbohydrates. He didn't eat his vegetables. Low sugar count ... no dessert tonight. That's unusual."

"Why?" O'Niel wondered.

"Because that's usually the only thing they serve in the worker's mess that's fit to eat." Another pause before she muttered, "No nicotine." A longer one before she said, "Some tranquilizers."

O'Niel leaned forward, trying to make sense of the squiggles filling the screens. "Tranquilizers? Are you sure?"

"Yeah." She chewed her lower lip as she fingered additional keys. "They're Company tranquilizers. Standard issue. Why the query?"

"Because the former owner of this blood was acting anything but tranquil not so very long ago."

"Yeah? He's plenty tranquil now." Her attention returned to the steadily lengthening columns of information. They continued to grow, but more slowly. The basics were known about the blue red liquid. Further analysis required more complex procedures.

"Blood sugar and hemoglobin are normal ... were normal. Nothing wrong with his brain, nervous system checks out." She frowned. "Hello."

"What?"

She seemed uncertain and her frown deepened. "I'm not sure. Funny."

Fingers fluttered above a different combination of keys, finally settled on a pattern. In the upper corner of the center screen a new pattern appeared. She touched additional keys. The pattern didn't change.

"Shit."

She tried still another combination, then shook her head in frustration.

"What's the matter?" O'Niel asked.

"Such a smart piece of equipment," she gestured at the console, "and a wreck like me trying to run it." She nodded toward a fourth screen. It was alight now, but blank. "That's where I want it to come up."

"Want what to come up?"

"Whatever it is. Take it easy. I'm not through yet." Again her hands played with the keys and buttons. The fourth screen remained blank.

Finally she leaned back in her own chair, crossed her arms, and spoke without taking her eyes from the brightly glowing columns filling the center three screens.

"You know, you don't have your medical all-star here, O'Niel. Company doctors are like the old-time ship doctors. Most are one shuttle flight ahead of a malpractice suit. A decent physician isn't going to come way the hell Outland to someplace like Io where it's cold and lonely. Not when she can stay home and buy twenty acres outside of Suva or Ponape to work out of."

"Something's there, isn't it?" He was pointing at the glowing screens.

"Maybe. Just maybe." She uncrossed her arms and attacked the keys once more.

"I spend my days dispensing tranquilizers to the workers, uppers to management for their amusement . . . yeah, I know that's illegal. So what? You gonna arrest me?" He didn't react to the challenge. She rambled on, still working the console by touch and trial.

"Also certifying that the Company prostitutes don't have syphilis. Take two aspirin and call me in the morning. That's a doctor joke, remember? I'm a doctor joke." She glanced up at him, the lines in her face deepened by the dim light.

"I don't know how to analyze a new molecule, O'Niel. My sights never ranged that high and my abilities don't range that deep."

Unexpectedly, the fourth monitor came alive in rebuttal. A diagram appeared, grew slowly as an invisible electronic hand traced the three-dimensional graphic. Lines and colored orbs formed a geometric abstract, though the computer's intention had nothing to do with art.

"Hello again," she said, a bit more cheerfully.

O'Niel was straining to see past her, his brain trying to make some sense of the little colored globes and bonding lines. He suspected what the diagram represented, but he couldn't be sure. His dealings with volatile organic compounds were usually on a less microscopic level.

"Is it a drug?"

She looked over at him approvingly, nodding affirmatively. "You just won a prize."

"What kind?"

She inspected the fourth screen, noting the information spelling out beneath the slowly revolving graphic. Various atomic combinations lit up in sequence within the molecular model, corresponding words and figures below the diagram grew in size and brightness.

"Some kind of narcotic for sure. Nothing I've ever seen before, and I've seen some cuties. You'd be surprised what gets smuggled in to a place like this past the Takeoff security . . . no, come to think of it, I guess you wouldn't be surprised.

"Synthetic, this one. Hate those things. You never know what they stand for." A last knot of multihued globes and bonds materialized, completing the molecular chain. The computer beeped, signifying that it was through. Simultaneously, the numbers and words beneath the diagram froze and two new words appeared, pulsing softly.

"Bingo," she said quietly. "Polydychloric Euthimal." She shook her head in wonder at the extremes of mortal man. "Those stupid bastards are taking Polydychloric Euthimal."

"That tells me nothing."

She swiveled around to face him. "It should tell you a helluva lot. Polydyeuth's an amphetamine. Strongest damn thing you ever saw." Her face flashed a falsely broad smile. "It makes you feel wonderful."

"Wonderful enough to override the effects of the Company tranquilizers he'd been taking?"

Sagan's name hadn't been mentioned, and it didn't seem necessary. "Strong enough to override anything," she snorted. "You do fourteen hours work in six hours, that kind of nonsense. Especially manual labor. It makes you want to work like a horse.

"The Army tested it a few years ago. I remember reading about it in a journal. It made everybody work, alright. Then it made them psychotic. It takes a while. Ten, eleven months, maybe more. Then the body starts paying for it.

"It fries your brain. They always told us in chemistry that you never get something for nothing."

"You said it was a synthetic." She nodded. "Can it be made here?"

"No. Impossible." She gestured at the quiescent analyzer. "The hospital staff's the only equipment on this rock sophisticated enough to deal with complex organics. You want physical or geologic analyses, there's half a dozen departments that can help you out.

"But organics? Uh-uh, no way. And we're only equipped for analysis here, not manufacture. We import even the most basic drugs.

"Besides which, even if it were possible, I'd

know. This isn't your everyday garden-variety narcotic. It takes real chemical know-how and a big, expensive lab setup equipped to deal with unstable organic compounds. There's no such animal on Io."

O'Niel's brain did not move nearly as fast as the computer's, but just then it was churning ahead at a pretty respectable clip.

"No autopsies, so nobody knows anything," he murmured. "The workers are producing more on the same amount of work time, so the mine is more productive. They get fatter bonus checks and the work seems easier, so they're happy. Nobody mentions anything about awkward little side effects."

"Like scrambled heads," she said quietly.

"Exactly. By the time their brains pop, their tour is up. Usually . . . except for the embarrassing early-bird blowouts like Sagan and the rest, and they're chucked out toward the asteroids in a hurry.

"The Company is making a bigger profit, so they're not about to ask any questions. They can claim ignorance by not trying to peek under the covers, and make it stand up under a truth serum." He was nodding slowly to himself. "That's not a bad setup."

He stood, headed for the door. "Listen, don't say anything about this to anyone. Not the analysis, not even that I was here tonight. Understand? *Anyone*. Somebody's gone to a lot of trouble to keep this real quiet. If it comes down to a question of keeping it quiet, I doubt whoever it is would show much respect for the medical profession."

"Like I said, I'm not stupid." She watched him open the door, and added rapidly, "I did good, didn't I?" The hardness was gone from her voice. "For a wreck."

"Yes, you did good. Real good. And a wreck couldn't have done it."

He smiled, a rare occurrence lately. It was warm, and genuine. Then he was gone, the Hospital doors closing tightly behind him.

Lazarus stared at the silence, then turned tiredly back to the still glowing screens. The molecular chain still turned slowly on the fourth monitor, pivoting patiently on its invisible axis, its makeup and composition laid out neatly in rows beneath the graphic. She had neither the experience nor equipment for identifying such a complex protein, yet there it floated, complete and exposed.

She hadn't thought to smile back at O'Niel, but with no one in the room to see, she allowed the long-dormant grin of satisfaction to slowly spread across her face . . . .

It was the same imitation coffee, perked with the same imitation caffeine, but for some reason the black goo tasted remarkably good this morning.

O'Niel sipped on his third cup and watched the computer begin to untangle the night. He hesitated before entering, looking down into his cup. It was blacker than space outside.

I'm getting addicted to this stuff, he mused. Maybe the rumors are right and it really is a petroleum distillate. I wonder what else the Company sticks in it?

That was a disquieting thought. He turned his attention back to the waiting computer. At least it wasn't imitation. If not the coffee, he knew he could always depend on his regulation electronics.

O'NIEL, he entered instinctively. W.T. CONFIDENTIAL. QUERY FORTHCOMING. SCRAMBLE. SECURITY PRIORITY, MY EYES ONLY.

The machine responded promptly. O'NIEL, W.T. PROCEED.

He typed in: DEPARTMENT HEADS WHO HAVE WORKED ON IO FOR MORE THAN A ONE-YEAR TERM?

That question produced four names. A nice, low number. One that shouldn't require much checking.

COOPER, FREDERICK—ADMINISTRATION
MONTONE, KENNETH R.—SECURITY
LAZARUS, MARIAN L.—MEDICAL
SELWAY, MARY—FOOD SERVICES

Then the follow-up: DEPARTMENT HEADS WITH MOST ACCESS TO MOST AREAS AND PERSONNEL?
Again a quick reply.

ORME, CHARLES—TRANSPORTATION
TRINGHAM, DAVID—PAYROLL
MONTONE, KENNETH R.—SECURITY
LAZARUS, MARIAN L.—MEDICAL
SHEPPARD, MARK B.—LEISURE AND ADMINISTRATION
O'NIEL, W.T.—SECURITY

He smiled at the appearance of the last name on the screen and lit a cigarette. For several minutes he did nothing except study the screen and indulge the habit. Then it was time to punch in the un-nice questions.

NUMBER OF EMPLOYEES WITH CRIMINAL RECORDS?

The computer took its time. O'Niel found himself nodding. It was only to be expected, on Io.

SEVENTEEN, was the response. O'Niel typed more.

NAMES, ALPHABETICALLY.

The computer instantly printed out the list.

ALABIN, THOMAS R.
ANDERSON, WILLIAM G.
BANDO, DOMINIC R.
DE PAUL, RAYMOND F.
DUMAR ROBERT E.
FOSTER PETER F.
FREYMAN, MARIN E.
HALPERN, GEORGE R.
HOOPER MARK G.
KUNARD, FREDERICK C.
LOOMIS, CHARLES E.
MONTINEZ ELVIRA T.
SPOTA, NICHOLAS P.
STEVENSON, JOAN A.
THOMPSON, VIRGIL
WOTTON, MICHELE G.
YARIO, RUSSELL B.

He studied the list intently. The names remained only names, did not match up with faces. That could be quickly remedied. Of course, if the next question happened to generate a blank, he would have to go back to square one.

BREAKDOWN OF OFFENSES, he entered. HOW MANY FOR DRUG RELATED CRIMES?

The computer went quiet and he found himself holding his breath. The pause was no longer than normal. It only seemed that way.

The console hummed.

SPOTA, NICHOLAS P.
YARIO, RUSSELL B.

WHO DO THEY WORK FOR? he asked, rushing the entry so fast he had to clear the screen and do it a second time.

SPOTA, NICHOLAS P.—LEISURE
YARIO, RUSSELL B.—SHIPPING

Oh, now that was interesting. He allowed himself a slight smile and his fingers flicked the keys.

WHO APPROVED THEIR EMPLOYMENT?

Machine, delightfully: SHEPPARD, MARK B.

O'Niel's fingers tapped rhythmically on the side of the keyboard, then moved once again across the keys.

TRANSMIT LIKENESS SPOTA, NICHOLAS P. AND YARIO, RUSSELL B. QUIET SEARCH. The last was so that some curious personnel clerk would not notice that his records had been scanned.

The screen blanked for a moment, still humming as it sent commands through the interlocking electronic nexus that linked every department at the mine.

Before long a man's face appeared on the screen in front of O'Niel. There were two views, straight-on and profile: the standard employee ID poses. It was a heavy-set, moderately ugly face, devoid of expression. Somewhere in his early forties, O'Niel decided. Tough, experienced, and unimaginative. That was a description that could apply to ninety percent of the men and women who worked at the mine.

Underneath the picture was the legend: YARIO, RUSSELL B.

The second picture O'Niel thought he recognized was of a man who moved around quite a bit, from department to department. He was about the same age as Yario, leaner and darker, if not prettier.

O'Niel studied both pictures, memorizing the two faces. Then he touched a special button and entered something other than a question into the computer.

REQUEST AUTOMATIC DISCREET SURVEILLANCE YARIO, RUSSELL B. AND SPOTA, NICHOLAS P. ALL SECURITY CAMERA REPORTS CONFIDENTIAL. MY EYES ONLY. O'NIEL. W.T.

The machine responded dutifully: AFFIRMATIVE

He entered, END TRANSMISSION and the computer acknowledged END TRANSMISSION, O'NIEL, W.T.

Three sections of the mine generated more power than they used. The first was the solar power station, which supplied the entire outpost with life. The second was the fusion backup reactor, which was rarely brought into use.

The third was the Club, which was never quiet.

. The woman dancing in the transparent cylinder beneath the baleful glare of the shifting strobe lights was not quite naked. The light wisps of material draped around her were placed more to satisfy convention than comfort.

She was gyrating wildly to a thunderous, ostinato rhythm blaring from the speakers set in ceiling and wall. Much of it was electronic, most of it percussive. Her head was tilted back and her teeth were bared in a cross between an erotic sneer and a laugh. Her hair, clinging to the nape of her neck, was matted with perspiration.

The cylinder was suspended above a long, curved bar against which men and women, offshift from the mine, bumped and swirled. Some watched the dancer in the plastic tube; others drank but most talked, glad to be out of their suits and breathing the illusion of real air.

A second cylinder floated at the other end of the bar. In it a man wearing even less than his young female counterpart twisted and spun. Muscles rippled across his body with every turn. Perspiration flew from his skin as he flailed at the air.

After a while the two cylinders began to move toward each other. Opposing panels slid aside and the cylinders merged. So did the two dancers, who never stopped moving. They executed a variation, prompting comments from those watching underneath. The man and woman knew many variations—they were professionals.

The people in the crowd were shouting, not in anger but simply so they could be heard above the roar of the music. Individual tables were packed tightly on the floor, lit by the amber fluorescents that glowed above the bar, providing most of the light that illuminated the Club, along with the energetic strobes that teased the dancers.

Circulating among the off-duty workers were the Company cleared "recreation assistants." Sometimes men walked arm in arm with men, women with women. Choices were limited enough by nature. Variety was not frowned upon, prudishness having been left behind somewhere inside the orbit of Luna.

A tall, well-dressed man ambled into the Club, peered over the heads of the swarm, and headed toward the distant bar, searching through the crowd as he broke a path.

One of the bartenders smiled at him. The man grinned back, nodded once. The bartender turned to his console and punched in the code of Spota's favorite drink. The electronic mixologist lit up like a pinball machine as it started on Spota's request, blending it in sequence together with two dozen others.

Hidden from casual sight among the exposed guts of wiring and air conduits overhead was a small tube not much larger than a pencil. It was painted to match its surroundings and whirred softly as its business end traversed the crowd.

O'Niel rested in his chair before the bank of video monitors and studied the multiple images they proffered. One screen showed an empty access corridor, another a panorama of the bustling cafeteria. The Club was on the third screen, the view changing slowly as the camera swept left to right.

When it reached the bar, O'Niel suddenly became alert and leaned forward. He jabbed at a switch, halting the camera's movement. Carefully he backed it up, nudging it down a notch until it was focused on a certain section of the huge counter. Then he touched the zoom control and held it down. It provided a close-up of Spota, who was accepting his drink from the bartender.

Brief conversation between patron and server was exchanged and then the bartender took Spota's ident card and entered it into the bar's computer. The machine would dock the drinker's credit line proportionately.

Spota's face flashed in the reflected strobe light as he looked upward. The dancers had separated and returned to their respective cylinders, which once more hung above different ends of the bar.

The girl was jiggling almost directly above Spota. O'Niel resisted an urge to direct the camera upward, kept it and his own attention resolutely on the glistening face of the man below. Spota was experienced. O'Niel could not risk looking away. He might miss something.

He was certain there would be something worth not missing.

The locker room echoed to the greetings and complaints of the night shift, returning from the mine. Some of the men already had doffed their helmets before exiting the elevator, a violation of Company rules and a direct challenge to death, which waited patiently just down the elevator shaft. Others hopped around on one foot or the other, half in and half out of their atmosphere suits.

These were dumped in large, dusty piles. They would be gathered up by clean-up crews and checked out for potential leaks, rips, and other assorted, potentially fatal little defects before being returned to their owners.

Nearby the morning shift was lined up patiently at the oxygen fills, each man waiting his chance to stock air. It was crowded when Spota entered the area.

O'Niel sipped at a cup of coffee that was too hot and winced. The autoperc in the squad room needed adjusting. Of course, he'd been working it overtime this past night.

He rubbed at his eyes as he watched Spota make his way through the piles of discarded clothing and down the aisles. The ceiling camera panned to follow its quarry.

Spota paused a few times to chat with some of the returning workers. Then he reached a

locker, opened it, and began climbing into his
own atmosphere suit preparatory to going Outside. O'Niel considered the brief conversations
he'd just witnessed. It was clear that Spota was
well-liked by his fellow workers. That befitted
someone who worked in Leisure and could
command all sorts of extra perks denied the
average miner—perks which might be shared
with good friends.

He noted the buttons Spota thumbed as he
entered the elevator, had a camera waiting
for the man when he arrived at Level
Eight. Spota's face was visible through the
faceplate of his helmet. The thin zero-pressure camera built into the scaffolding moved
to follow.

Spota stopped to talk with some of the men
and women, ignoring others. None of the busy
workers told him to get lost, despite the fact
that such conversations cost them work time.
Spota was evidently more than merely well-
liked by his colleagues; he was downright
popular.

O'Niel ground his teeth and wished fervently
for an audio override that would enable him to
listen in on the suit-to-suit channel Spota was
using. It would be useful sometime, he told
himself, to learn to read lips.

He could always store the surveillance
camera's recording and refer it to someone
who *could* lip-read, except that most of the
time Spota's face was turned away from
the pickup's eye. So he had to be content
with merely watching. It was very frustrat-
ing.

Dust always managed to work its way into the shuttle loading dock. The cavernous chamber was full of sulfur dust and often smelled like a Texas barnyard at high noon in early August. Tan and yellow sulfurous clouds drifted around workers and machines as heavy containers of ore were bullied into place.

One of the shipping operators was using a yellow lifter to straighten a line of ore carriers. A soiled bandana encircled his forehead, damp with sweat. Like everyplace else in the mine, excepting certain private quarters and the administration offices, the dock was under-cooled.

The name of the individual manipulating the lifter was Yario. He looked big enough to man-handle the ore containers by himself. Hair the hue of the local coffee tumbled down the back of his neck. A tattoo of a striking serpent undulated on his left arm as the muscles beneath twisted and strained.

O'Niel watched him work, noting his attitude and skill as he handled the lifter. He wasn't as quick with the complicated machine as some of the others, nor as smooth, but he did not make any mistakes.

The Marshal's attention bounced back and forth between two screens: talk and load, load and talk. Spota and Yario. It was going to be a long day.

The Club was never quiet, never closed. Like the miners, administrative flunkies, and service personnel there were different shifts of bartenders, dancers, and prostitutes. New dancers performed old steps and ancient bumps and grinds to the beat of fresh music.

O'Niel's cameras changed to follow Yario into the Club, where the overhead pickup latched onto him. As he watched he chewed mechanically on a sandwich of three slices of soy-based "meat" trapped between two slices of real bread. Like O'Niel, the wheat was a long way from home.

He reached out and adjusted the zoom switch. The ceiling surveillance camera closed in on Yario but did not exclude from pickup those workers joking, drinking, and dancing immediately next to him.

The shipping operator finally confronted a tall, smiling brunette. They immediately commenced negotiations. Io had no time for subtleties.

Spota, meanwhile, had completed his outside tour and was on his way to the showers. The camera tracked him as O'Niel struggled to stay conscious.

Later he watched Yario wolf down breakfast. Something had to break soon, he told himself. It had too, and it's likely to be me, O'Niel told himself.

He picked at the remnants of the previous night's sandwich, attempting to masticate a stale mouthful. On screen, Yario continued to down his food, shoveling it in. O'Niel's mouth turned damp. The food looked wonderful.

Morning turned into afternoon. Spota played some pinball and filled out a few reports, while

Yario pushed ore around. O'Niel's eyelids felt like lead.

Night again, the Club teeming with customers, the music tapes changed again and the dancers endeavoring their best to change steps to match it. People packed two and three deep around the bar.

Yario was walking down a passageway, Spota down another. O'Niel used a wet washcloth on his face. Both men walked on out of range of their respective cameras. The images on the two monitors flickered uncertainly for a few moments, then shifted automatically to new pickups.

Spota entered the Club. So did Yario, from the rear entrance. O'Niel tossed the damp cloth aside, shook his head to clear it.

Shoving his way through the crowd, Spota made his way toward the bar where he opened conversation with a male prostitute. Yario, sitting at an empty table, was soon joined by a redhead. Interesting, O'Niel thought absently, how people always differ from what you expect. He would have picked Spota for the ladies' man. He welcomed such surprises. They kept him wary.

About an hour, he guessed. It was actually some five minutes sooner when Spota escorted his date across to the table where Yario was sitting. The foursome ordered drinks and chatted amiably.

Workers swirled around the table, one spilling a drink on Yario, who displayed admirable restraint in simply ignoring the incident. To

O'Niel's mind, that made the big man that much more dangerous.

So far everything had gone about as he'd expected. Two new figures came into camera range and joined the foursome's conversation. One of them was Sheppard. That was a bit of a surprise, since the Club was such a public place.

The other was Montone, which was a shock.

O'Niel's body tensed as his eyes left Yario, left Spota, and ignored Sheppard. He concentrated on the other new arrival: no question but that it was the sergeant.

While Spota and Yario stood making excuses to their intended dates, the camera tracked to follow the four men as they moved to a table at the rear of the Club. As soon as all were seated they launched into an intense conversation, leaning close to one another so as not to be overheard.

O'Niel's fingers drummed on the side of the keyboard. His lips were pressed tightly together.

The conversation didn't last long. Spota and Yario left the table first. As per instructions the overhead camera moved along with them. O'Niel hurriedly activated a second monitor and locked it on the table where Sheppard and Montone continued to talk.

O'Niel kept watching them, ignoring Spota and Yario for now. Eventually Sheppard rose, left Montone alone at the table. O'Niel left the pickup running, forced himself to turn his attention away from the sergeant and back to his two principal subjects.

The workers' quarters provide little privacy and even less relief for the men who must enter the mines each day.

The mine workers fill their oxygen tanks preparatory to entering the exterior mine shafts.

**Federal District Marshall William Thomas O'Neil (Sean Connery)
searching for hired killers who have been sent to Io to assassinate him.**

Dr. Lazarus (Frances Sternhagen) tends to O'Neil's wound after he has been shot by a hired gunman.

Workers don helmets and backpacks before entering airlock door and mineshaft elevator.

Con Am boss Sheppard (Peter Boyle).

O'Neil and deputies try to lure crazed worker out of a bedroom where he is brutally attacking a prostitute.

Sheppard (Peter Boyle) practices golf swing on a simulated computerized fairway in his office.

Hole 18   rds Par 4

Police squad room and communication center.

O'Neil checks his messages on television communication monitor as wife
Carol (Kika Markham) prepares breakfast for son Paul (Nicholas Barnes).

O'Neil in administrative wardroom asking for help from Con Am executives in apprehending ringleaders of drug operation.

Connery puts on space helmet before entering airlock and outside confron-
tation with assassin.

Two hired assassins prepare weapons after arriving on Io via the space shuttle.

O'Neil and wife Carol embrace as he leaves his office.

O'Neil unbolts access corridor to get to assassin inside.

Spota (Marc Boyle) followed by O'Neil walks through locker room to drug-drop with mine workers.

O'Neil begins to chase Spota through workers' quarters.

Spota leaps across corridor in an attempt to escape from O'Neil.

Spota attempts to kill O'Neil in mining complex kitchen.

O'Neil disarms Spota and subsequently busts him for drug possession and smuggling.

They'd returned to their former table, where their respective dates awaited them. Montone sat by himself for awhile, nursing his drink. Eventually O'Niel cut him off . . . .

VII

The ball slammed off the smooth wall and rocketed toward the back of the court. It was larger and heavier than a normal tennis ball, and the racket O'Niel attacked it with was latticed with extra-strength nylon cable.

The ball flew toward the rear of the twenty-foot high court. Gray sweat shirt and pants flapping, Montone lunged at the ball just in time to undercut a return. O'Niel played in shorts and old track shoes and moved as though slightly possessed, assaulting the ball as if it were a live enemy only he could destroy.

Both men were perspiring freely, their jittery figures nearly lost within the comparative immensity of the scuffed white court. Despite the expanse and heavier ball, the low artificial gravity still made the ball relatively easy to chase down.

Neither player exhibited much skill. Montone was slightly older and more experienced, relying mostly on spins and position. O'Niel, on the other hand, simply mugged the ball and attempted to overpower his opponent.

The sergeant anticipated the location of his boss's next return and was able to slice the ball out of reach. O'Niel started for it, then slowed when it was clear he'd never reach it in time.

"Shit," he muttered, hands on hips. He turned to await Montone's serve.

"Nine seven." The sergeant dumped the ball high off the front wall. O'Niel went high to get it, followed Montone's diagonal return with a cut to a corner. Eventually the Marshal won the point.

Breathless, he bent over and put his hands on his knees, fighting to get his wind. Montone ambled over, breathing equally as hard.

"You going to tell me about it?" O'Niel asked his sergeant abruptly, between gasps. "Or are you going to sit on it all day?"

Montone said nothing, handed the ball over, and returned to his line. O'Niel served it hard to his right but Montone blocked it, lifting a return nigh off the wall that make the Marshal leap for it.

"Tell you about what?" the older man asked.

O'Niel just managed to get his racket on the ball. His return was feeble, leaving Montone an easy put-away which he lofted softly into an unreachable corner.

"Sheppard," the Marshal said.

Montone's face paled slightly. He bounced the ball a few times, not acknowledging his partner. Eventually he served, putting a lot of backspin on the ball.

"What do you want to know?"

The serve didn't fool O'Niel who was ready and waiting for the backspin. He grunted with the effort as he powered the ball back toward the wall.

"How deep are you in?"

Montone used a kick off the side wall to gain leverage and chopped the ball upward, putting topspin on it this time and trying to richochet it off the ceiling.

"Not too deep."

"How deep is not too deep?" O'Niel held his position close to the front wall, waiting for the ball to descend and slamming it floorward. Montone lunged and hit it to the far side.

"I'm paid to look the other way."

"I get it." O'Niel was content just to return the ball. "You don't do anything bad, you don't actually help. You just don't do anything good. Right?"

Montone didn't answer as he countered the shot, but his expression was pained.

O'Niel continued. "I'm going to bust Sheppard."

That brought a louder response from the sergeant; one of disbelief. "Are you serious?" He sliced the ball wickedly into a corner, cutting the velocity sharply.

"Yes." O'Niel dove for the dying ball and just missed it. He rolled over on the floor, panting hard and not in any hurry to get up.

Montone used the opportunity to try and regain his own wind. "This isn't the place for heroes. There's no publicity value to a big bust out here, no promotion and raise waiting for you if you succeed. Which you won't." He shook his head slowly.

"You try to bust him, you're messing with more than you think."

O'Niel slowly climbed to his feet, balanced his racket in the palm of his left hand while gripping it hard with the right. He stood and waited for the next serve. Montone bounced the ball, staring sideways at the Marshal and waiting for a comment.

"You going to serve or not?" O'Niel asked him.

With a weary frown, the sergeant whacked the ball toward the distant wall.

"You're talking about the General Manager here," he said urgently, "not some penny ante pusher out to make a few bucks on the side. He's a real hot shot with the Company . . . I know, he's shown me his commendations."

I bet he has, O'Niel thought tightly.

"You're talking about big money," Montone went on. "You're talking about people and places that we only know of from letterheads, and people who never use letterheads because they don't want to be known."

O'Niel missed the return, turned and poised himself patiently for the next delivery. Montone didn't bounce the ball this time but just stood on his line and turned to face the Marshal. A pleading tone crept into his voice.

"I've got to warn you, the guy's connected,

and to more than just the Company. I mean it. There's some serious stuff involved. Heavyweights. The kind you don't want messing around in your territory. Don't fool with them and they leave you alone. That's better all around."

O'Niel looked sharply at him, his expression unchanged. "Better for whom?"

Montone sighed, bounced the ball once, and spoke while gazing at the floor. "I don't understand you, Marshal. Busting Sheppard. What would it prove?"

O'Niel returned his attention to the forward wall, still waiting for the next serve. "I'm not trying to prove anything."

"Aren't you?"

"No. I gave up trying to prove things a long time ago. But I've got to stop this, and I'm going to.

"First of all, I don't like Sheppard. I don't like his face, I don't like his voice, I don't like him, period. Second, this stuff they're selling is killing people. I don't much like that either."

Montone kept his eyes on his feet. He was still breathing hard, sweat dripping from his chin, and his gray sweats stained dark.

"What are you going to do with me?" he muttered.

O'Niel looked over at him, considering. Finally he said quietly, "I honestly don't know."

"You want me to resign?"

"No." He thought another moment. Both men stood quietly, one waiting, the other debating with himself.

Finally O'Niel reached a decision. He'd known men like Montone before, just marking time until retirement, trying not to get in anybody's way, working hard to avoid stepping on important folks' toes. Montone wasn't evil—just weak.

"Don't come between me and Sheppard," he told him. "Don't tell him anything, don't mention this conversation or the fact that I know what's going on. Just take your money and look the other way. Do for me what you're doing for him. I don't want you. You're small fry. I want him."

Montone swallowed, his words barely audible. "I'm sorry I didn't turn out better."

O'Niel was staring at the wall. "So am I."

"My wife was no dummy." Montone's knuckles were white where he gripped his racket.

"Your serve," O'Niel said curtly.

Montone readied the ball, smacked it solidly toward the wall. O'Niel pounced on it furiously . . . .

Yario's fingernails were black with dirt and grime. He drew the back of a hand across his forehead just above the encircling bandana, then put the lifter back in gear and started it forward.

O'Niel divided his attention between the view on the monitor and the paperwork that glared at him insistently from another screen. It wasn't hard to watch Yario while working on the bureaucratese. The latter was mostly routine stuff. It kept his mind busy.

Clouds of ever-present dust swirled in the

lights of the busy loading dock as massive lifters and cranes wrestled with the next cargo
load of ore. Men and women shouted to be
heard above the rumble of machinery.

A familiar shape strode into the loading area,
walking down a long aisle of ranked containers.

O'Niel's hands left the keyboard as he turned
his full attention to the two monitor screens.
Spota, heading for Yario's lifter, walked right
past it without so much as glancing up toward
its operator.

Several minutes passed before Yario finished
aligning the ore carrier he'd been shifting,
then touched switches. The huge armature
stopped, the engine grinding to a halt. He
swung himself down and started off in Spota's
wake.

Puffing on a fresh cigarette, O'Niel watched
patiently. He'd been watching for a couple of
days now, and eventually the monitors would
show him what he'd been waiting for. O'Niel
tried hard not to get excited. He'd been disappointed before.

Spota turned down another aisle and
stepped behind a row of containers that placed
him beyond the overhead camera's line of
sight. Yario had been walking faster now and
was just behind him. Neither man reappeared
immediately.

Cursing the positioning of the surveillance
camera, O'Niel leaned forward toward the
screen.

Yario re-emerged first and Spota let him get
a fair distance away before re-entering the

light. They walked off in opposite directions. Neither said a word to the other or exchanged any sign of recognition. Yario returned to his waiting lifter while Spota strolled casually out of the loading dock area.

O'Niel played with the keyboard and controls, filling the center screen with the view from first one monitor, then another. At this critical moment he didn't trust the automatics to keep track of Spota. The man made his way through a succession of access-ways, greeting those he knew in passing as though nothing unusual had happened. Which it hadn't.

There was one frantic moment when Spota entered one accessway interchange and failed to appear on the other side. It took O'Niel several minutes of hectic manipulation before visual contact was re-established. Spota was now strolling down access corridor Twenty-seven. That was fairly close to the Security section.

Close enough, O'Niel suddenly decided. He was fed up with watching screens.

Grabbing the stubby riot gun from the rack behind his desk he tore out of the office, ignoring the startled salute of the deputy on station.

Spota continued on his way toward the locker room, blithely unaware he was now being tracked by something less tenuous than a video monitor. O'Niel had already assumed that was his intended destination and where most of the exchanges were likely to have taken place.

Of course, if Spota was fast enough, he'd be

able to dump whatever he was holding into one of the disposal johns and face the Marshal with clean hands and dirty smile.

At the moment there was nothing to induce Spota to take such reckless action, nothing to hint that today would be any different from the smooth routine of the previous day or previous weeks. The man continued deliberately on his way, only occasionally pausing to smile at a passing acquaintance or customer.

O'Niel nearly knocked down the woman who was walking in the middle of his accessway. He was running full speed now, faster than he'd pursued the racket ball. The woman yelled after him but he didn't hear her curse, having already rounded the next corner.

Spota reached the hatchway leading to the mens' locker room, opened it, and walked inside. He made his way past the video stations, past the lockers, past men dressing and undressing, past the oxygen fillup station where the next shift was finishing topping off prior to going Outside.

O'Niel reached the hatchway half a minute late.

Spota's progress through the room was slow, impeded by men coming off work who were in the process of removing their bulky atmosphere suits. He didn't shove or push but took his time working a path through them.

The hatchway slid aside with maddening slowness, though its reaction time was no slower than usual. It only seemed that way to O'Niel. He charged into the locker room, hesitated, searched the aisles anxiously. A few of the men looked up curiously from the noisy video screens, their eyes going wide at the sight of the riot gun.

Spota was nowhere to be seen.

Those workers who noticed the gun threw questions at O'Niel. Ignoring them, he ran the length of the locker room, peering intently down each aisle in hopes of catching a glimpse of his quarry.

In the congested aisles it was difficult to tell one man from another. If Spota had planned his arrival for maximum concealment he couldn't have chosen a better time than shift changeover.

Easy, O'Niel admonished himself, take it easy. They have no idea anyone knows anything about their operation. There's no reason for Spota to suspect and take evasive action. Unless Montone talked. He doubted that. The sergeant wasn't a doer.

Spota turned a corner and started down another aisle. O'Niel saw him just as he disappeared behind another row of lockers. The Marshal meandered through the busy workers, still ignoring questions, not caring who he bumped out of the way.

A few of the miners elbowed aside turned to protest but most of them shut up when they saw the Marshal's bars on O'Niel's collar. The more pugnacious shut up when they got a glimpse of the riot gun.

A younger worker far down the aisle had opened his locker and was stowing his work gear. He did it indifferently, not caring where the sometimes sensitive electronic components were placed. Most of his attention was devoted not to undressing but to the men up-aisle from his locker. He was evidently expecting someone.

That someone was Spota. A flicker of recognition passed between the two. The younger man continued undressing, his movements becoming even more casual. His thoughts were not on his work.

O'Niel was breathing hard, only half the length of the aisle behind Spota now and gaining on him with every step. His gaze lifted, went beyond his immediate quarry to the worker undressing at the locker. He saw how the man's eyes were searching up-aisle, saw the desire flaming behind them. It was a look the Marshal had encountered before, in the faces of people who purchase certain substances. The worker was about to buy something, and he was going to buy it from Spota.

That still confident individual was barely a step away from his waiting customer when O'Niel bumped into a man who happened to be crossing the middle of the aisle.

"Hey, buddy, why dontcha look where the hell you're . . . oh, sorry, Marshal. I didn't know it was . . . ."

O'Niel tried to quiet the man but it was already too late. The commotion caused Spota and his customer both to look up the aisle. They recognized the Marshal immediately.

Spota lunged forward, throwing his customer aside, slamming him hard against the metal wall of lockers. O'Niel cursed once and charged after him.

The dealer had lost any vestige of composure and was like a wild man, banging his way down the aisle without a care for who or what he bounced off in the process. O'Niel would have shouted at him to stop save he couldn't spare the wind. He muscled his way in pursuit, trying to catch up to his man without maiming any of the puzzled bystanders in the process.

Spota had no particular place to run. At the moment his sole concern was getting away from the Marshal. O'Niel knew that if the man did so there were plenty of places for him to hide within the mine complex. A clever associate would then have no trouble getting him shipped safely off the moon no matter how thoroughly O'Niel would try to check all outbound cargo.

Then it would be back, not as far as square one, but a lot further than he wanted to be. It had taken O'Niel days of patient surveillance to bring him this close to an actual exchange, to a point where he knew his man could be caught with the goods on him. He'd be damned if he were going to start all over again.

Besides, the opposition would know now that he knew what was going on. Discreet surveillance would be ten times as difficult, and he didn't want to risk that.

And there were other things to worry about. Montone's concerns were no doubt justified. O'Niel had no intention of giving the opposition a chance to regroup.

He couldn't let Spota get away.

Noise and confusion shadowed both running

men. Voices rose and fell in the locker room; uncertain, worried, puzzled, frightened. Only rumor moved faster than Spota and the Marshal.

The dealer jumped onto a bench dividing an aisle, grabbing an open locker door and pulling himself up. Keeping low, he started making his way across the vast chamber by leaping from one row of lockers to the next, thereby avoiding the congestion below.

O'Niel followed, grunting with the effort as he pulled himself upward. By the time he stood atop the lockers Spota was nearly halfway across the room. The Marshal hurried after him. Spota's agility was already taking a toll.

Once O'Niel tripped and would have split his face neatly on the unyielding metal if he hadn't caught himself in time. Regaining his footing, he grimly jumped to the next aisle in line.

Spota threw himself from the last row of lockers, tore into an access corridor beyond the locker room. His eyes blazed with a mixture of fear and rage. He ran like a caged animal recently escaped.

He'd nearly reached the end of the corridor when O'Niel appeared at the other end. Clawing open the hatchway, Spota disappeared beyond without trying to close it behind him. O'Niel muttered to himself. If Spota had spent a minute trying to close the hatch, the riot gun could have cut his legs out from under him.

Leaving the hatchway unsealed after use

was violation enough to haul the man in on, but O'Niel had other charges in mind. He hurried onward.

His mouth was working hard as he swallowed air. The lightweight corridor tube swayed under his weight. Only a man experienced in deep-space work could keep his balance in that jiggling passageway. Support ribs flashed by like highway signposts.

Where the hell is the bastard headed, the Marshal thought worriedly? Does he even know? They were close to the main cafeteria now, but that would be crowded as always. It was a likely, familiar place for someone to run to, but the crowd inside would make escape difficult and ditching the polydyeuth almost impossible. Spota was running wild, but not blindly.

The other corridor beyond the hatchway led to the liquid storage dome. O'Niel turned up it, praying he'd guessed right. As he entered the open hatch at the far end he had the satisfaction of seeing Spota racing along the thin inspection catwalk twenty feet above the first tank. He didn't slow to congratulate himself.

He didn't want to use the riot gun unless he was forced to. He wanted Spota in condition to chat. In any case, some of the liquids stored in the dome were chemical catalysts, others acids and volatiles used in the mine. Not a good place to throw shells around, even at a low-velocity setting.

Maybe Spota knew that also, because he showed no fear of the gun haunting his back as he started down the ladder descending the first tank.

O'Niel was now on the overhead catwalk, watching as his quarry jumped from one series of steps to the next. He hurried over the side onto the ladder.

Spota now started up the metal rungs mounting Tank Two, taking the steps several at a time in the reduced artificial gravity. By the time O'Niel reached the base of the first tank, Spota was already on the second catwalk, increasing the gap between them.

But he was running out of options. O'Niel forced himself up the stairs to the second catwalk, running as fast as he could. Starting down the second flight of rungs on the far side, Spota headed for the ground-level hatchway. O'Niel followed, almost stumbling and falling from the landing atop the tank to the floor below.

Another accessway, this one leading upward. Another hatch, then a second. Spota was not thinking anymore or he would have considered hiding somewhere. But he could only flee madly. If only he could get a full corridor ahead, get out of O'Niel's sight.

He looked back over his shoulder, gasping for air as he worked the hatchcover at the corridor's end. It opened ... and there was O'Niel just entering the far end behind him, silent and implacable as ever. With an inarticulate cry, Spota plunged through the opening and into the bustling cafeteria, unmindful of anyone or anything that got in his way. Anger had been left behind and panic drove him now.

Trays and food went flying as he bowled over a cutter, then a crane operator.

O'Niel entered the rear cafeteria portal. As he'd expected and hoped, the repeated collisions had slowed the fleeing dealer down. There was no time to stand there watching. He rushed into the dining area. He could hardly breathe. His throat was raw and his heart pounding as he stumbled red-faced in pursuit.

But Spota was tiring, too. His agility had enabled him to increase his lead over the Marshal in the open corridors and storage dome. In the packed confines of the cafeteria it was the bulkier O'Niel who had the advantage.

He hurled himself into the crowd waiting in line for food, flailing with arms and elbows. One man went down with blood pouring from his mouth, reaching angrily for his assailant. Spota was already halfway down the queue.

O'Niel was too angry and tired to smile. He was used to working his way through crowds, and knew he had gained on his quarry.

Spota glanced over a shoulder, saw the expressionless Marshal coming closer with every step. The cafeteria exit was packed with off-shift workers arriving for lunch. He looked frantically to his left, then right. There was a doorway. Anywhere unblocked, his brain shouted at him!

He vaulted the food service counter with everyone trying to get out of his way. One unlucky cafeteria server wasn't so fortunate

and had the tray of steaming food she'd been
carrying thrown at her head.

O'Niel leaped the counter, avoiding the injured worker lying on the ground holding her
face. There was nowhere for Spota to go now
except through the double metal doors into the
kitchen.

Spota stumbled past the rows of microwaves,
the steam tables, and cauldrons of ready-mix
food. He could hear O'Niel's footsteps now.

Too late, he realized he'd closed himself in.
The far end of the kitchen was coming up
toward him, a maze of tubes, wiring and piping
decorating the wall beyond. He wheeled
around. O'Niel was nearly on top of him.

A vat of boiling water simmered nearby,
awaiting the next crate of frozen vegetable soy.
Groping inside his shirt, Spota's fingers seized
the vial of red liquid taped there. He threw it
into the vat.

O'Niel never hesitated. He'd come too far,
worked too hard for this moment to hesitate.
He shoved his hand into the water, his teeth
clenching around a dull groan of pain. His
fingers felt the vial, closed around it. As he
pulled it out he saw that the plastic had been
warped but not melted. The red fluid inside
still sloshed freely, uncontaminated by outside
agents.

It gave Spota the seconds he needed to grab
the long butcher knife and bring it down toward O'Niel's arm. The Marshal threw himself
aside and the blade slammed into the metal
rim of the vat.

Holding the riot gun by the barrel he swung

it at Spota, who'd raised the knife to take another stab at his tormentor. The stock caught him on the shoulder, deflecting his thrust so that the point of the knife barely pierced O'Niel's forearm. Blood instantly started to seep through the shirt.

They were close enough to grapple. O'Niel tried to get a lock around Spota's neck, but the man was as wiry as a cat. He kept lashing out with legs and knife. It was all O'Niel could do just to keep from being cut again.

This won't do, he thought exhaustedly. He brought his knee up and Spota doubled over. O'Niel rolled to his left. Spota lurched to his feet and started toward him again, waving the knife.

The riot gun went off four times in rapid succession, shattering lights, plastic utensils, and packages of food. In the confines of the kitchen the quadruple thunder was deafening.

Spota froze, the knife still ready to stab. The four blasts had struck in a circle around him, but he was untouched. The gun, however, was now pointed significantly at his forehead. The four blasts had come so quickly they'd seemed to be echoes of one.

O'Niel was kneeling on the metal, panting hard and holding the gun ready in one hand. The other arm dripped blood onto the food-stained floor.

"Think it over," the Marshal said quietly.

Spota considered the speed with which the four shots had been fired, the neat circle the four blasts had formed around him. He stood there, the knife ready, watching the Marshal. The gun hand was as steady as the dome protecting the kitchen.

Slowly, reluctantly, he let the knife drop to the floor . . . .

VIII

Containment was located deep inside the jail, past the offices and the squad room. O'Niel strode down the narrow corridor, past large transparent windows on which were stenciled the words: NO ARTIFICIAL GRAVITY

Zero-gee containment was a relatively recent development in law enforcement. It's hard for a man to make trouble when he's weightless. Gravity is an ancient ally of the troublemaker. Without it, he loses confidence as well as leverage.

The cells were unpressurized, each having its own small airlock. Prisoners wore special security atmosphere suits. Instead of individual tanks, air came from a central source via long tethers affixed to each suit, that further ensured the docility of prisoners so confined. Even if you could make trouble in the absence of gravity, the comparative fragility of the air supply kept disturbances to an absolute minimum.

Several cells were currently occupied. Two fighters brooded opposite each other, unable to do more than glare through faceplate and windows. In another compartment one of the mine's more boisterous drunks was sleeping it off peacefully, floating in emptiness.

O'Niel checked them out as he made his way down the corridor, favoring his bandaged arm. There were two different dressings, one for the knife wound, another for the burn. He was glad Lazarus hadn't been on duty when he'd entered the infirmary for treatment. No doubt she would have treated him with some choice comments between the disinfectants and the bandaging.

Montone trailed after him.

"How's the arm?" His tone was subdued.

"Better. Still hurts. Where is he?"

"In thirty-seven," the sergeant informed him.

"Has he said anything?"

"Not a peep. The only time he's opened his mouth is to accept food."

"Anybody ask about him?"

Montone's voice dropped to a disconsolate mumble. "No, no one. Not yet, anyway."

"If anyone does, I want to know."

Montone hesitated, ventured a weak smile. "That goes without saying, doesn't it, Marshal?"

O'Niel glanced back at him, swallowed what he'd been about to say. There was nothing he could say that would make Montone feel worse, and nothing the sergeant could say to make his superior feel any better.

They halted before cell thirty-seven. Beyond the window Spota drifted at the end of a long red tether. O'Niel automatically checked the gauge which monitored the flow of oxygen through the tube. It held steady. Then he activated the intercom receiver set on the wall between the air flow valves.

Stenciled on the window next to the small airlock was the message: CAUTION — ZERO ATMOSPHERE — OXYGEN REQUIRED

O'Niel lifted the small transceiver, spoke toward it while observing the suited figure floating inside the cell. "Spota, this is O'Niel."

The only response was the sound of steady breathing. Spota had to listen whether he liked it or not, O'Niel knew. Speaker and pickup were built into the same helmet that was supplying him with air.

"Okay, keep quiet," O'Niel said. "I'll do the talking for awhile.

"We just got the lab report back on that vial you tried to scald. It's very interesting. Want to know what it said?" Still silence at the other end of the line. "It says you were carrying four ounces of Polydychloric Euthimal. Four whole ounces.

"That's four hundred doses. That's a lot of junk for one man to be hauling around, Spota. Bad junk. Let's see . . . four hundred doses; that ought to get you about four hundred years. You won't be an old man when you finish out your sentence, Spota. You'll be dead. Even with time off for good behavior, you'll be dead. Not that your bosses could care. You're just a cipher to them. Unless we can come to some kind of mutually beneficial agreement."

When he finally spoke, Spota's voice was distorted by the low-level speaker. "I don't know what you're talking about, Marshal."

"Of course you don't," O'Niel said pleasantly. "You're just an innocent, ignorant bystander. You thought you were carrying around a vial of wine. Tell me something. How much does Sheppard pay you to market the stuff? Work as rotten as this ought to at least pay well."

"I don't know what you're talking about."

O'Niel's expression tightened, though his tone didn't change.

"You're a real tough guy, Spota. I'm impressed. You're not going to have any trouble staying in there. Most people start to go a little crazy after a few nights, though, because they start dreaming about not being able to feel the floor." He leaned against the glass and smiled so that Spota could see him clearly.

"Sometimes the tether gets knotted and a man suffocates. You tend to spin in zero-gee when you're asleep. That doesn't happen very often, of course. It's just that the thought of it sometimes keeps people up at night." He paused, letting the image soak in before continuing.

"Except, you're a tough guy, Spota. So that possibility won't bother you."

"Piss off, Marshal."

"That's what I like, Spota. Someone who's real quick with a comeback. Someone who's sharp as well as tough." He growled at the pickup.

"You know what, Spota? I'll let you in on something. I've got you nailed. I got the evidence, I got the witnesses. Never mind the assault, resisting arrest, attempting to destroy evidence, running hatchways without sealing them behind you, conspiracy and all the other little goodies you tacked onto yourself during that little jaunt through the station the other day. Those are just frosting.

"You're going to be shipped back to the main trans-Jovian station on the next shuttle and do time that makes this look like a picnic. Eventually they'll get a writ to feed you truth serum and get the answers that way."

"Admissions made under truth serum aren't admissible as evidence in court," Spota countered, sounding a little less confident.

"A jailhouse lawyer, too. Now I'm really impressed," O'Niel told him, not sounding impressed at all. "Technically you're right, but the boys at the main station will find some way to make it stick. They always do.

"They'll make a special effort in your case, Spota, because the stuff you're peddling kills people. That makes certain folks real mad. Oh, they'll make everything stick, all right. You're going to do time that'll make this seem like a vacation.

"And Sheppard? Sheppard will shrug and bring in a new flunky and get a little richer. So don't make a deal with me. Don't get a reduced sentence. Be real noble and take the fall. Just do your hard time while Sheppard laughs his

ass off at you. I've seen it happen like that
before, dozens of times. Each time you hired
punks think you're doing something special.
And the bosses love it, because they always
come out winning." He took a deep breath.

"I've got to hand it to you, Spota. You're
pretty sharp. See you around, tough guy."

He hung up before Spota could reply even if
he'd wanted to. Let him simmer in his own
thoughts for awhile. Maybe he'd come around.
O'Niel's hand still stung from the burn treatment. He turned to Montone.

"Nobody talks to him. Nobody comes near
him. I mean *nobody*. Do you understand?"

"I understand," was the slow reply. O'Niel
headed for the exit. "Where are you off to
now?"

"That's about enough hard work for one
day," was O'Niel's reply. "I think I'll visit some
friends . . . ."

The room was large and dark, mellow with
recessed lighting that enhanced the richness of
the paneling on the walls. Comfortable black
vinaleather furniture was tastefully deployed
on the thick gray carpet. There were pictures
on the walls and one isolated sculpture set on
its own illuminated lucite pedestal.

At the moment the heavy imitation wood
desk was nearly bare. Even the computer terminals that were built in were sheathed in
warm wood tones.

Sheppard stood in the middle of the office,
putting the golf ball into an automatic return.
With each successful putt the machine announced his score, the distance traveled by the

ball, and the speed of the putt. Then it gently blew the ball back to him.

When Sheppard missed, one of two long arms would swing out in a wide arc until it contacted the errant ball. With a hook and twist, it would guide the ball back into the returner which would then plonk it back to its owner.

The twin arms didn't have to work very hard. Sheppard was quite good. The result of much practice.

He studied the undulating carpet as a voice issued from inside his desk. "He's here, Mr. Sheppard."

The General Manager lined up another putt from a fresh angle. "Let him in."

There was a soft hiss from the far end of the room as the door slid aside, admitting O'Niel. If he was impressed by the luxurious surroundings he didn't show it.

Sheppard didn't look up to greet him. He stroked the putter, watching as the ball hooked into the waiting cup. The machine hummed and announced the result.

"Quiet," Sheppard ordered it. Obediently it turned off its audio system. The Manager moved to his right, tapped the ball gently.

"You know," he said conversationally, "I can hit a seven iron five hundred yards on this place. An atmosphere suit doesn't give you much mobility, though. Your swing suffers." He gestured toward the gleaming, well-stocked bar, alive with crystal decanters and glasses. "Fix yourself a drink. The booze is real."

"No thanks." O'Niel stood quietly in the diffuse light, waiting.

Sheppard used the end of the putter to move the ball around on the carpet, trying to decide which angle to try next. "You've been busy."

"So have you."

The Manager tapped the ball again, moving it close to a chair leg. His voice didn't change as he asked, "How much do you want?"

O'Niel didn't reply.

"How much?"

The Marshal lit a cigarette, inhaled deeply. The pungent smoke whirled lazily roofward until the cleaning equipment plucked it out of the air.

"That's what we need here," Sheppard murmured disgustedly, "a goddamn hero." He sounded tired. He missed the putt, strolled around to a new position.

"This floor was originally set level. I had parts of it raised and the carpet reset, just a little, just enough to make things interesting. Golf and life are always more interesting when they're tilted just a little, don't you think?" He bent over, squinting.

"I think this piece of rug has a slight break to the left. Listen, O'Niel. Let me tell you what you're dealing with here. I run a franchise. The Company pays me to dig as much ore out of this hell-hole as possible. There's one of me on every mining operation in the system.

"My hookers are clean and good-looking and don't cheat their tricks. My booze isn't watered, my dancers are the most attractive and enthusiastic, and I see to it that the tapes and music for the locker room players are changed every damn shuttle flight.

"The workers are happy. Don't take my word

for it, ask them. Ask any multiple tour man or woman who's worked here. Io stinks, but the mine doesn't.

"When the workers are happy, they dig more ore, and get paid more bonus money. I don't take a slice of that. Anything they earn they keep. I get my own bonus checks. When they dig more ore, the Company is happy. When the Company is happy, I'm happy."

"Sounds wonderful," was O'Niel's laconic comment.

"Nothing here is wonderful," Sheppard countered. "It works, and that's enough. Every year we have shift changes. Every year a new Marshal comes in to do his tour. They all know the score. You know the score. You're no different. If this hero routine is to get your price higher . . . I'll think about it."

O'Niel said nothing, spent several minutes strolling around the sumptuous office. Sheppard finally looked up from his putter and eyed him with genuine curiosity.

"What are you after?"

O'Niel concluded his inspection. It had cost more to furnish the office than he made in a year. He stared evenly at the General Manager.

"You."

Sheppard sighed and displayed a sad smile as he returned to his putting.

"What is it with guys like you? If you were such a goddamn super cop, what the hell are you doing on a Company mining operation like Io? They didn't send you here as a reward for your sterling service. You know that and I know that." He stroked the ball.

"I read your record. I read everybody's records before they're assigned here. You want to know why the hell you're here instead of being a Captain somewhere on some nice Earth-side beat like Singapore or New Perth? I'll tell you why. It's right there in your record, if not in so many words. But there are lots of little hints and clues. I'm good at reading that kind of stuff.

"You've got a big mouth. That's why you're sent from one toilet to the next. But you've made your choice about what you want to do with your life. That's your business. Just don't step on mine because I don't plan on spending the rest of my life doing what I'm doing now."

"Good for you."

Sheppard's cajoling tone turned to one of exasperation. "I could understand if this were going to get you somewhere, but it can't. This charade of yours is silly, pointless. Also inconvenient for me or I wouldn't give a damn. You try and meddle, you better know what you're meddling with. You got something to prove, prove it to yourself."

O'Niel turned to leave. "See you around."

Sheppard's voice rose slightly. "If you're looking for more money, you're smarter than you look. If not, you're dumber than you look."

O'Niel smiled back toward him. "I'm probably a lot dumber."

"That can get very dangerous."

O'Niel was still smiling as he left the office.

It was night but O'Niel couldn't sleep. He rolled over and flipped on the reading light. The apartment was dark, quiet. He sat up in bed. The sheet next to him was unmussed, the section of mattress untouched. He'd spent too many years on his own side of the bed to roll over onto the undented part. The empty part.

He climbed out of bed, methodically dressed himself. The apartment remained vacant, the emptiness of it shouting, screaming at him. If he couldn't sleep he'd work.

The bustle in the corridors helped to wake him, but it vanished as he neared the security section. Only the mine worked double shifts. Administration was asleep.

There was no one inside the squad room to admit him. The night shift deputies were all out on patrol. It wasn't necessary to waste manpower by having someone simply sit inside. The machinery would greet visitors, answer questions, refer problems via remote units to the scattered deputies.

He stuck his Ident card into the gaping slot. There was a brief delay while the computer checked it. Then the door beeped politely and slid aside.

The lights were dimmed. Everything was clean and neat, awaiting the return of human workers. He started toward his office, thinking to check the evening's reports to the hour. His feet shifted and took him instead toward the cell area. Maybe Spota would feel more like talking now.

As he made his way down the narrow access corridor he routinely checked each cell. The corridor itself was dark, lit only by the pin lights glowing above receiver units and air controls. The two fighters had been discharged, a different cell was occupied. O'Niel checked the card gripping the wall. Another drunk. He moved on.

The cells themselves were brightly lit. All of the prisoners were sleeping, their biological clocks unaffected by the artificial illumination. The lighting was for the benefit of the jailors, not the prisoners. Anyone who wanted to sleep could darken his helmet faceplate.

In the dim corridor you had the sensation of walking through an aquarium. O'Niel would far rather have been looking at fish. Inhabitants of the type that usually frequented such cells had long ago ceased to have much interest for him.

Except one, the speciman in cell thirty-seven.

Some of the prisoners floated sideways while others lay curled in fetal positions. The experienced lawbreakers favored spread-eagle posture because it kept you from spinning too much in your sleep.

O'Niel halted at the last cell and lifted the receiver.

"Okay, Spota. You've slept on it long enough. It's time to talk."

As stubborn as ever, he thought, when there was no reply from the other end of the line. Spota drifted with his backside toward the glass.

"Hey, tough guy."

Still no answer.

"Hey . . . ." O'Niel's voice trailed away as he pressed his face to the glass and stared into the cell.

The oxygen tether leading to Spota's suit had been severed, both neatly parted ends floating freely in the zero-gee cell. A trickle of pulpy blood leaked from the section of tether still attached to Spota's helmet. Tiny red globules bounced lazily against the cell ceiling, the floor, and gathered in corners.

O'Niel's face twisted and he made an ugly sound as he slammed a fist against the glass. Then he was running, down the corridor, out through the empty squad room, out into the main corridor and back toward Admin living quarters, a single thought in his mind, laughing at him.

Montone.

The door did not respond to O'Niel's repeated requests for entry. There was a chance the sergeant was somewhere else, but there was no need for him to hurry. He probably thought O'Niel was still in his own apartment, asleep.

He used a card pick to fool the door seal, exploded into the room, his face flushed, his breathing hard.

A quick scan showed no one in the apartment. The simple furnishings appeared undisturbed.

"Montone!"

There was no answer. He moved to the sergeant's bunk and saw that it hadn't been slept in. There was one other place before he headed for Sheppard's rooms. He walked angrily across the room and pounded on the bathroom door.

"Montone . . . are you in there? It's O'Niel. By God, if you're in there it'll go better on you if I don't have to drag you out!"

Still only silence.

He started checking out the room, pulling open desk drawers and dresser compartments.

Clothes and personal effects were still neatly stowed in their respective compartments. That he hadn't expected. Unless Montone was in such a hurry to find a hiding place while awaiting the next shuttle that he hadn't bothered with them. So where the hell had he gone?

O'Niel had a new thought, crossed the room and jerked aside the closet door . . . and found Montone.

The dead man's eyes protruded from his head. His tongue hung limply from a corner of his mouth, swollen and black. A wire garrote was imbedded in his neck. One end was fastened to the closet. The sergeant's hands were tied behind his back, the same grade of wire cutting deeply into the skin.

O'Niel stared a moment longer, then took a deep breath and reached into the closet. Eventually he unwound the wires and wrestled Montone's limp form to the floor. Terrified eyes looked past him toward the ceiling.

He looked around the room and found the bunk. Pulling off a sheet, he used it to cover the corpse, and then moved to the intercom to call the hospital.

When he finally returned to his own apartment he was more numb than tired. Above the computer console the green message light was winking.

Turning, he walked over to the station and slumped into the chair and wearily fingered the keys.

O'NIEL, W.T. MESSAGES?

The machine hummed brightly. O'NIEL, W.T. AFFIRMATIVE.

He touched additional keys.

PLAYBACK

MESSAGE FOR O'NIEL, W.T. YOUR EYES ONLY/CODED. ENTER CLEARANCE CODE

A little of the depression lifted from his brain as it was replaced with curiosity. Now what the devil was so important it had to come in coded at this time of night? He struggled to remember any code-relevant instructions he'd programmed into the console.

The machine accepted his code, replied quickly. SBVD DTKKHRCY. JBTFWPA.

"Fascinating," he muttered to himself, then typed in: DECODE. MY EYES ONLY.

The machine's reply was brief, but said a lot: FOOD SHIPMENT ARRIVAL — MONTONE.

That dissolved the last vestiges of sleepiness. ELABORATE, he ordered the console.

It only repeated, FOOD SHIPMENT ARRIVAL — MONTONE.

The hell with elaboration, he thought determinedly. The short message might be eloquent enough. He turned off the console and started for the door. Out in the corridor he found himself slowing, thinking.

Montone didn't want to know, didn't want to think, he reminded himself. It got him dead. He increased his pace to a trot once more, but changed his direction. It wouldn't hurt to make the detour.

The entrance to the loading dock was unwatched. He touched the hatchway control, watched it slide aside for him. As he entered

the dock he switched on the tiny flashlight. It
thew a thin shaft of white illumination out into
the dark jungle of equipment and containers.

He moved in, closing the hatch behind him.
The light led him down the ramp between a
pair of motionless lifters. There were no shifts
on duty at the moment and his own heartbeat
thundered in his ears. Places that are normally
noisy take on a nervous quiet when they're
unoccupied. The larger the place, the louder
the silence.

It took him a few minutes to locate the containers which had arrived on the recent shuttle.
Patiently he inspected the markings on each
crate and cylinder. The light hopped from one
seal to another, finally settling on several massive containers with ribbed surfaces. They had
cold-seal markings stamped on their sides.

Another console had supplied him with
names and numbers. He checked his hastily
scribbled list as he moved from one container
to the next. There weren't many and he soon
located the one he was after stamped with the
Company logo, the cold-seal warning, and the
words REFRIGERATED/PERISHABLES.

The locking latches were tougher to break
than most because the container was temperature as well as pressure sealed. Eventually they
gave in to his insistent pressure and snapped
open.

A gust of frigid air rushed out. O'Niel waited
for the imprisoned breeze to subside; then he
bent over and entered the container.

There was enough room inside for him to
stand erect. His exhalations created small

clouds in the freezing air. His shirt cuffs were
pulled down to his fingers and his collar was
turned up and buttoned in place for extra pro-
tection from the deep cold.

Sides of beef hung from large hooks, shiny
red beneath the pale layer of frozen fat. It
reminded O'Niel of hospital morgues. The rigid
rank of beef sides ran the length of the container. Most of them would find their way to
the Administration kitchen, then to the plates
of managers and assistants. The workers would
see little of it.

He started to work his way down the line of
gutted carcasses. We've something in common,
he mused, studying the beef. We're both a long
way from home.

His light danced off protruding ribs. He
wasn't sure what he was searching for, but
knew that he'd recognize it when he saw it. So
far there was nothing.

Until the wire slid over his head with a faint
whitt of passing air to lock around his throat
before he knew what was happening. The wire
tightened immediately, beating O'Niel's hands
to his neck.

He clawed at the wire, but it was locked
tight around his throat and almost cut through
the tough nylon of his shirt. There was no
room, not room enough to get fingers or even a
fingernail between it and his neck to stop the
pressure, the cutting, choking pressure. He
fought for breath.

Yario was no rabbit, like Spota. He was a
big, solid bastard and he'd done this kind of
work before. His knee pressed firmly into

O'Niel's back, lifting the Marshal off the floor and arching him backward. O'Niel's feet kicked helplessly in the air.

His eyes were bulging wide and he was making harsh, rasping noises as he fought to break Yario's grip. He swung a few futile blows with his elbows. They bounced harmlessly off Yario's massive sides, as did the feeble kicks he attempted with his feet. Yario's face was red with the effort and the garrote dug into his own hands, but he didn't let up on the pressure for so much as a second.

Slowly, gradually, O'Niel's movements grew weaker. The muscles in his neck ceased to stand out. His arms, then his legs stopped moving. So did his chest.

Yario took no chances, though he knew from experience the Marshal couldn't be faking. Not with the kind of pressure being placed on his esophagus. When he was sure O'Niel was dead he let go of the garrote. The weight against his knee went completely limp, crumpling against him.

He let the body drop to the floor of the container. So much for the Marshal. He wouldn't interfere any more. There wouldn't be many questions. Lots of people held grudges against lawmen. A place like Io would be alive with potential killers. The fact that Marshal and sergeant had died so close together would be explained away as an awkward coincidence. Or something.

That wasn't his problem. He'd leave the explaining to Sheppard and the Company. Yario was no deep thinker—he just did his job. Did it well, as O'Niel and Montone could both attest. Or rather, couldn't.

He grinned at the thought, stepped over the crumpled shape and headed for the far end of the container. The individual sides of beef were stamped with their destination. A few read CAFETERIA. Most read WARD ROOM MESS. A very few were directed toward individuals.

At the back was one stamped GENERAL MANAGER. Yario grunted with satisfaction and started to turn it around on its supporting hook. He was getting chilly and in a hurry to be on his way.

O'Niel's leap sent him slamming into Yario's rib cage. The startled larger man was thrown off-balance into the container wall, the force of the impact momentarily knocking the wind out of him. O'Niel brought up the heel of one palm and drove it into the bridge of Yario's nose. There was a cracking sound and blood flew, congealing rapidly in the chill air of the refrigeration container.

Yario staggered forward like a wounded bear, thick arms outstretched to gather in and crush his assailant. O'Niel gave him credit for overcoming his pain and surprise. He wasn't about to give the massive machine operator a chance to recover any further.

Bending low, he drove forward and put his head into Yario's solar plexus. The air went out of the huge body with a *whoosh* and it doubled over. As it did so, O'Niel put all his weight behind the knee he swung up to catch the man's descending chin. The impact echoed dully through the container and spilled out into the shuttle dock.

Yario went down without a sound and lay quietly on the floor—as quietly as the sides of beef hanging suspended around him.

O'Niel stumbled backward, leaned against the cold wall for support, and tried to catch his breath as he stared down at Yario. The man wasn't faking it, as O'Niel had. He'd be unconscious for some time, for which O'Niel was grateful. A dangerous opponent, much more so than the panicky and now very dead Spota.

Reaching up with one hand, the Marshal unbuttoned his high collar, the rigid protective neck shield it had concealed still in place. With his fingertips O'Niel could feel the deep gash the garrote wire had cut in the tough plastic.

He unsnapped the collar and inspected it. If Yario had kept on pulling he eventually might have cut through the shield. But there was no reason to suspect its presence, so he'd let loose as soon as he'd thought the Marshal dead. Fortunately.

O'Niel tossed the collar to the floor and made certain the big man was definitely out. Anyone that big and quiet who knew how to use a garrote properly was someone O'Niel had no desire to wrestle with again.

Rising, he walked over to the side of beef Yario had been turning. With satisfaction he noted the words GENERAL MANAGER stamped into the meat. He began turning it slowly, as Yario had been doing, shining his own light on the frozen carcass. There seemed nothing unusual about it; no sewn-up cuts, no special markings.

Using the flat of his palm he tried slapping the beef, the sounds hollow inside the chilly container. He was starting to shiver.

Unexpectedly, a slap generated a *whick* instead of a thick, flat sound. Reaching into his pants pocket he withdrew a small knife. It was an old-fashioned folding steel blade, not one of the fancy laser scalpels like those used in the hospital, but it would do. He sawed at the outer layer of fat where his slap had made the funny noise.

Once he'd made a hole of sufficient diameter he stuck his hand in, probed with his fingers. Before long his face broke out in a pleased smile. Using the knife again he sliced a long opening in the beef, peeling aside the outer layer of fat and meat.

Where the tenderloin ought to have been there was a hollow space. In the hollow, neatly stacked, were more than a hundred of the soft plastic bags of red liquid that Spota had been carrying.

His smile widened. Each bag looked as if it held about four ounces. Four hundred doses per bag. Forty thousand doses resting in the side of beef. That represented quite an investment on somebody's part.

It was up to him to see that the red death was properly filed. Generally O'Niel hated filing, but this job would be a pleasure. He looked around, found a sack full of tiny bottles of wine also marked GENERAL MANAGER. He dumped the wine, not caring if any of the bottles broke, then started transfering the plastic bags into the sack . . . .

IX

The fairway was bright green and recently groomed. Closely bunched cypress guarded the right side. Tufts of cloud floated in a sky of adamantine blue. Off to the left were several cleverly laid-out traps and a serpentine stream filled with lily pads. Additional bunkers were visible off in the distance, guarding the approaches to the Green. The distant flag marking the cup fluttered loosely in a warm breeze.

A loud crash sounded as the polished mahogany driver struck the ball. The ball flew a short distance before contacting the wall, at which point it fell to the floor. Its computerized image, however, flew onward from the exact spot where the ball had made contact with the wall-screen, the sensitive screen tak-

ing note not only of the angle of contact but
also the ball's velocity. Both had been trans-
fered to the computerized ball-image now fading toward the Green.

The image landed some two hundred forty
yards from the tee, off in the right rough. Sheppard pursed his lips as he studied the results of
his drive. He was still slightly twisted around
in follow-through posture. In a moment he
would touch the control that would advance
the scene toward him, automatically matching
up the real ball sitting on the fake grass by his
feet with the lie of the computerized image.

He stood alone on the false turf at one end of
the office. The rest of the work area was dark,
lit solely by the projected image of the cham-
pionship Gulf course glowing brightly on the
wall-screen.

"What's the matter?" a voice inquired solicit-
ously out of the darkness. "Sun get in your
eyes?"

Sheppard turned, lowering the club. O'Niel
stood at the far end of the office, silhouetted in
the doorway by back light from the reception
area. A smaller, feminine voice sounded
agitatedly from behind him.

"I'm sorry, Mr. Sheppard. I told him you
weren't to be disturbed but · he just
pushed . . . ."

"It's all right, Darlene. You can go." The slim
shape outlined behind O'Niel hesitated, then
disappeared.

"Well, well. If it isn't the law." Sheppard
calmly returned his attention to the screen and
concentrated on setting up his approach shot.

"I'm working on distance right now, not accuracy. It's not a bad lie. What do you think ... a seven iron?"

O'Niel walked into the room, closing the door behind him. "Hey, Sheppard. Guess what I just found in a meat locker? Fresh off the last shuttle and waiting for pickup down in the loading bay?"

"I have this feeling you're going to tell me even if I don't guess." He spoke while selecting an iron from his golf bag.

O'Niel continued, thoroughly enjoying himself. "I found two hundred fifty pounds of hamburger named Yario that works for you. I also found your new shipment of PDE. I threw the hamburger in jail and the PDE in the toilet. Or was it the other way around? I've got the hamburger's cell locked and me with the only combination, so he doesn't have any naughty visitors while he's sleeping."

Sheppard's fingers tightened on the shaft of the iron. He turned slowly to face O'Niel and tried to smile. The effort failed. His tone was softer than usual.

"My, you've been a busy little Marshal, haven't you?"

"Are you proud of me?"

"Let's say I'm truly dazzled."

He turned back to the screen, lined up and swung. The ball sliced low and to the left, hooking badly. Both men watched in silence as the ball-image landed in the near trap. Sheppard's hand was shaking ever so slightly as he turned to jump the screen image forward.

"Nice shot," said O'Niel approvingly.

Sheppard adjusted the control, brought the image too close, backed it slowly until a red light beeped at him from the tiny wall-screen control console, signifying that the real ball lying on the false grass by his feet matched up with the image that had been on the screen. He tapped the ball gently with the end of the iron.

"Did you really destroy the entire shipment?"

"Yes. Quite a lot of it, wasn't there? Business must be good. Good enough to drive at least a hundred men and women to suicide before you'd have to reorder."

"You *do* have a flair for the dramatic."

"No, actually I prefer to go about my work quietly. Tell me, was it expensive?"

"More so than you can ever imagine." The General Manager had recovered his aplomb.

"Hard to replace?"

"Harder than you can ever imagine."

"Looks like you're out of business, then."

Sheppard deliberately took his time putting the seven iron back in the bag. The cost of shipping golf clubs and the comparatively useless bag all the way to Io had been considerable. Sheppard reached for his wedge, paused a moment to study the Marshal the way an entomologist might study a new species of butterfly.

"I think I've misjudged you, O'Niel. My first impressions were all wrong, and that's unusual. You're not stupid. You're crazy."

He pulled the wedge clear of the bag, spoke pityingly but not sympathetically. "Do you really think you've caused anyone more than an inconvenience? An expensive inconvenience, I grant you, but only an inconvenience. Is that really what you think?" He shook his head sadly.

"Go home and polish your badge, Marshal. You're dealing with real grown-ups here. You're out of your league. Can't you see that? Can't you understand what you're doing to yourself?"

O'Niel's slight smile didn't disappear. "I bet whoever sent you that shipment is going to be mad you lost it. Real grown-ups don't have much of a sense of humor about such things." He looked past the staring Sheppard, to the image glowing on the wall-screen.

"I'd use a nine iron here. Just try to swing easy. The trap doesn't look too deep. But if you're not careful you'll bury yourself real quick."

He turned and headed for the door. Sheppard started to take the shot, paused to look toward the departing figure.

"Marshal."

O'Niel halted, but didn't look around.

"You're dead, you know that? Dead. You hear me?"

"I hear you." He continued on out of the dimly lit office without looking back . . . .

O'Niel made his way through corridors and accessways to the lower levels of the mine. The lower he went the fewer people he met. Machinery lived in the depths of the complex, machinery that ran itself and often repaired itself. Only rarely was the attention of its human builders required. Maintenance was routine, performed at predetermined intervals.

Occasionally unscheduled adjustments had to be made to certain pieces of equipment. O'Niel descended the last walkway, turned to his left after briefly consulting a small map. He hoped to make one such adjustment.

The hatchway he soon encountered was marked ELECTRICAL BAY. He unsealed it, hefted the small black case in his left hand, and walked in, careful to seal the hatch behind him.

The bay resembled a mausoleum, a low-ceiling endless chamber filled with row upon row of vertical islands. Each island contained the wiring and relays for a separate section of the mine.

A soft hum of power disturbed the air, flowed through the room. It was energy drawn from a distant sun used now to serve the needs of humans and other machines.

O'Niel made his way past several islands, constantly refering to his map. As expected, he was alone in the bay. The islands varied considerably in size. Some were quite massive, such as those for the male worker's quarters, female worker's quarters, and the mine lifts. Others were smaller, such as the one marked HOSPITAL. Eventually he found the one labeled GENERAL MANAGER SYSTEMS.

Rows of metal panels lined the islands like the scales of a fish. Communications fibers ran from island to island, thin strands of glass wrapped in opaque plastic. There was a small slit atop each panel. O'Niel located the one he

wanted, slipped his special security ident card
into it.

A row of multi-colored lights blinked once,
then stayed on. The panel snapped open, ex-
posing an intricate nexus of wires, glass fibers,
power lines, and the familiar colored geometry
of printed circuits.

He studied them carefully, his gaze traveling
from one to the next. The power leads he ignored.

Eventually he located a thick cluster of shiny
glass fibers. The spider's nest marked the confluence of multiple communications lines, private lines, interspatial, and computer linkups.
Working by number and code he painstakingly
traced several of the lines until he found the
one he wanted. Then he opened the small case
he'd been carrying.

The interior was a sloppy mass of wires and
chip boards; tools rested somewhat more neatly
in a side compartment. O'Niel selected a thin
piece of insulated glass fiber with transparent
end links. Carefully he placed one end across
the fiber leading to Administration. The other
end he set against an empty terminal inside the
panel marked MONITOR.

As soon as they made contact, both blunt
ends of the short cable annealed to the terminal and cross fiber, forming smooth, unbroken
joints. Their special chemical composition
would not interfere with the laser-boosted messages flowing through the communications fiber.

Since there was no distruption of electrical
flow, only a slight lessening of light intensity

which would be compensated for at the next laser booster up the line, no one could tell that the communications fiber had been tapped.

He closed the panel, the snaps clicking into place. As soon as the final snap locked home the lights glaring above the panel went out. As shadows slumped down around O'Niel, he closed his bag, turned, and made his way back out of the bay. No one had seen him enter, and no one saw him leave.

The squad room was bustling with activity when O'Niel strode in the following morning. Most of the day shift deputies were already there, chattering among themselves, swapping stories as they awaited their new assignments. A few noticed O'Niel's arrival and nudged their neighbors. The level of conversation lowered but never ceased altogether.

It was Ballard who confronted him as soon as he arrived. The deputy kept pace with him as they crossed toward O'Niel's office.

"Good morning, Marshal."

"Morning. What have we got?"

Ballard thought a moment. "A breaking and entering in the women's quarters. Can't tell if it was a pervert, a thwarted lover, or an attempted burglary. Anyway, the guy was surprised and ran like hell."

"Any prints?"

"Nothing clear enough to record. I double-checked myself to ensure that was thoroughly processed, after what happened with that Sagan fellow. We don't want another guy like that running loose."

"I doubt that this is similar," O'Niel told

him, "or the guy wouldn't have run. Sagan wouldn't have. But your thoughts were right."

"I was hoping you'd say that. It didn't tie but a few people up and I thought it wouldn't hurt to make sure."

"Right. What else?"

"Not much. The usual drunks, the usual complaint from Ms. Machard in Admin about the peeping tom. Reports of a fire on Admin Level Two which proved to be false." He broke into a knowing grin. "Oh, yeah. There was a doozy of a fight in the cafeteria."

"Over what?"

"At first I thought it might've tied in with the breaking and entering in the female worker's quarters. Jealous boyfriend confronting a lover and like that." He shook his head. "Nothing so sensible. Somebody butted in line ahead of somebody else."

O'Niel gave him a disgusted look.

"Yeah, that's the way I felt. As if the folks stuck here don't have enough serious problems. Anyhow, it was more noise than substance. A broken nose and some teeth was the extent of the damage. Plus the breakage, for which their pay will automatically be docked." He gestured over his shoulder. "Both guys are cooling off in the tank."

O'Niel nodded his approval, then frowned. He was looking at Ballard's collar. "Where are your sergeant's stripes?"

Ballard looked uncomfortable. "Ah, well . . . Marshal, you know it's only been a couple of days since Sergeant Montone, and I thought . . . ."

"You're the new sergeant," O'Niel snapped, interrupting him. "You wear your new stripes or you're out of uniform. Understand? Put them on now."

"Yes, Sir."

Ballard went off to comply, leaving O'Niel to enter his office alone. The first thing he did was check the readings on Yario's cell. Oxygen flow and internal pressure were stable, the former higher than normal because Yario was bigger than normal. The bastard was still alive. O'Niel didn't consider going down the corridor. He'd learned his lesson with Spota. Yario wouldn't talk. O'Niel would leave him to the processors at the main station.

He sat down in front of the data console. Before checking in he took a moment to relax, staring out through the transparent partition at the assembled day shift.

They're a cheery bunch, he mused, surveying the deputies. Young, most of 'em. They think they're pretty tough, just like the miners.

They were on Io for the same reason as the miners: money. According to the personnel records most of them were married. Some had kids, though not on Io. He wondered how many would evaporate when push came to shove. Because it was going to, he was pretty sure of that. You didn't kick people like Sheppard in the butt without them trying to kick you back twice as hard.

Their faces were eager, expressions animated. Most of them enjoyed their duty. They were too young yet to be disgusted with it. He doubted many of them had ever confronted anything more dangerous than a raging drunk.

They haven't learned yet, he told himself. Probably most of them never will. If they're lucky.

He sighed, swiveled the chair so that he was facing the console, and punched in his code and name.

O'NIEL, W.T.

The machine challenged back: O'NIEL, W.T. SECURITY CODE?

He entered the code and the console responded: PROCEED.

MY EYES ONLY, he typed in. A quick glance showed that everyone was still gathered in the middle of the squad room listening to Ballard, who was reading out the assignments. There was no one standing casually next to the window.

SURVEILLANCE COMMUNICATIONS TAP ON SHEPPARD, MARK B. RESULTS TO DATE?

The wonderful thing about the security computer as opposed to a human deputy, he mused, was not only its speed of response but the fact that it never argued or talked back to you, or took up your time with useless questions. It just gave you the facts, ma'm, just the facts.

FOUR COMMUNICATIONS, the machine informed him. THREE INTER-OFFICE, ONE LONG DISTANCE.

Now that was interesting, he thought. Not entirely unexpected, but interesting. It seemed that Sheppard wasn't a man who was troubled by second thoughts.

DESTINATION OF LONG DISTANCE COMMUNICATION? he inquired.

The console replied: MAIN STATION, TRANS-JOVIAN SPHERE OF OPERATIONS.

REPLAY, he ordered.

A babble of incomprehensible noise issued from the moaning speaker set in the front of the console. O'Niel quickly jabbed the STOP button, keyed in the order to REWIND/UNSCRAMBLE/REPLAY.

The computer whirred as a tiny tape somewhere inside the console was respooled. There was static, then the sound of a com unit beeping to life. The small video screen also came alive. It showed Sheppard's face. The General Manager sat at his desk, looking into its pickup. He was evidently waiting for a reply to a call. He looked agitated and upset. O'Niel was pleased.

"Hello?" a strange voice said. Sheppard's image reacted instantly. He continued to look directly into his pickup, spoke as though conversing with O'Niel and not the unseen and as yet unknown greeter.

"Bellows?"

"Yeah, this is him," came the reply.

"This is Sheppard. We've got to talk."

On another keyboard O'Niel made an entry: BELLOWS — MAIN STATION TRANS-JOVIAN SPHERE OF OPERATIONS. TRACE.

"Goddamn right we do," the man named Bellows agreed belligerently. "What the hell has been going on over there?" He sounded upset. O'Niel's gratified smile widened.

"Just a little trouble," Sheppard told him.

"Your trouble is becoming big trouble," Bellows informed him gruffly. "You're getting some people upset who shouldn't be upset."

"What do you mean?"

"I mean that some people think you don't know how to take care of your own operation. From what I've heard lately I can't say I blame them."

"Tell them I can take care of everything. I just need to borrow a few of your best men for a couple of days. Just a couple of days."

"What about the two you had?" Bellows wondered. "I thought they were doing a good job?"

"They were . . . up to a point. They weren't the best. Send me the men and I'll get everything straightened out. I only need them for a little while, then they can go back."

Bellows mulled over the request, sounded reluctant when he finally replied, "My people are not going to like this."

"They want everything smooth again, don't they?" said Sheppard persuasively. "Then do it. Tell them I'll have it all straightened out fast."

"When do you need the men?"

"I want them on the next shuttle. The sooner the better, and the sooner everyone will be happy again."

There was a pause, during which Sheppard did his best not to squirm or look concerned. O'Niel thought the General Manager did an excellent job.

"I'll see what I can do," Bellows finally announced. "It won't be easy. They're hard to convince."

"Just a couple of days," Sheppard reminded him. "That's not much to protect the investment they have here."

Bellows agreed reluctantly. "I'll try. Call you back on this line later."

There was a series of rapid clicks, then static. Sheppard's image dissolved into electronic mush.

O'Niel played the conversation back in his mind as he stared absently out into the squad room. The deputies were gone, headed to their duty stations. So was Ballard, most likely to supervise a further check on the breaking and entering business.

He turned back to the console, typed in: RESPONSE TO SHEPPARD, MARK B. MESSAGE JUST PLAYED?

The console replied immediately: AFFIRMATIVE. RESPONSE 18:30 HOURS.

REPLAY UNSCRAMBLED O'Niel directed it.

There was more humming, more static, followed by the beep signifying that interspatial contact had been made. Sheppard's face reappeared on the screen.

"Sheppard here."

"This is Bellows," declared a now recognizable voice. "You've got the men you want. It wasn't easy. My people are very unhappy with you. This could cause trouble for them on all the other mining stations."

"I don't see how," Sheppard replied. "This is strictly a local problem."

"Like hell." Bellows made a rude noise. "If the Company got wind of what's going on out your way they'd clamp down on us like a vise. As long as our operations are run quietly, they'll leave us alone.

"But they can't afford any bad publicity. You know that. It could cost them their ore concessions. You know how this kind of thing would look if the media got ahold of it. It'd be the end of the Company's operations out here.

"That could put my people out of business, and my people like being in business."

"So do I," said Sheppard reassuringly. "Tell them not to worry. How good are the men you're sending over?"

"The best. That's what you asked for, wasn't it? Well, that's what you're getting. They'll be on the shuttle arriving there Sunday."

"They have their own weapons?" Sheppard's voice was very professional. He might as easily have been talking about the arrival of a dozen new lifters. "I can't afford to issue them any here. Too many questions would be asked. Too many people would know who might be asked awkward questions later on."

"They know that. You think you're getting a couple of dummies? These aren't lower-grade punks like Yario and Spota, you know. These guys are class."

O'Niel studied the screen, slowly rubbing his beard with one hand.

"They're bringing everything they need," Bellows went on. "All you have to supply are instructions. I'll pass them on. Then you sit back and stay out of their way and let them do their job, understand? Anything changes when they get there, they'll turn right around and come back."

"Don't worry about that," Sheppard assured him. "I've no intention of changing anything in mid-stream. I want this done and over with fast.

"As to instructions, the target here is O'Niel, the local Marshal."

"Jesus." For the first time Bellows sounded concerned instead of merely upset. "I thought it was some big-mouth miner or Admin assistant or someone who'd got wind of the operation. But the local Marshal . . . ." His voice took on a note of anger.

"I'm warning you, Sheppard, you better not mess this up."

"I won't." The General Manager was quite confident.

"Okay then. It's your party." Bellows sounded as though he didn't envy Sheppard the days ahead.

"Yes, it is."

"How much help will he have? Not that it would make much difference to the guys you've got coming over, but they ought to know."

"None."

"You sure?"

"Yeah, I'm sure." Sheppard smiled thinly at the pickup. "Nobody here will stick their neck out for anyone. Oh, during a fight at the Club, sure. Piss-ant stuff like that. But they're not stupid. They're all here to do their tour and get the hell out.

"It's just this one new Marshal who's causing all the trouble. The man's a mental case." The General Manager shook his head sadly. "Once the word is spread that these guys coming over are pros there won't be any trouble, and I've got somebody on the inside who will spread the word. Don't worry. He's a dead man. As dead as our temporary little difficulties here."

O'Niel ground out his cigarette in the ash tray, crushing tobacco and paper to a thin disk-shape.

"Sheppard, I've got to tell you something. Something you probably already know." Bellows' voice was level, noncommittal. "If this doesn't work, the next guys who come over for someone will be coming for you."

"No problem." Sheppard smiled at the screen, outwardly unconcerned at the threat. "If I didn't think it would go over smoothly I'd never have asked. Tell your people to relax. I'll call you when it's over."

There was a click, then static and mush. O'Niel folded his hands across his belly, leaned back in the chair and regarded the blank screen thoughtfully.

Time began to pass more slowly the next day, when the large digital readouts located throughout the mine started to come alive. They'd been provided for the enjoyment of the workers. Watching the various clocks count down the minutes was a pleasant way to pass some time in anticipation of the next shuttle arrival.

An incoming shuttle meant new films, mail tapes, private packages from wherever home was, new workers arriving, old hands with tours completed checking out: all sorts of delightful things.

This particular shuttle carried something more unusual and less delightful.

The double bulkheads outside the shuttle dock were cleaned and checked for leaks in anticipation of arrival. Over the main access hatch the readout announced: SHUTTLE LOCATION — STATION GREEN. The readout had remained unchanged ever since it had newly come to life.

Now it flashed anew: SHUTTLE — IN TRANSIT. ARRIVAL 70 HOURS 00 MINUTES.

Men and women crowded around the cafeteria tables noticed the readout above the serving counter as it came to life: SHUTTLE — IN TRANSIT. ARRIVAL 69 HOURS 58 MINUTES.

It didn't matter what section of the mine you were in; the readouts were everywhere, insistent and inescapable. You could see one from your bunk, from your station in the crater, in a corner of the video screens at the ends of the locker room aisles. Some professed to see the countdown in their sleep.

And if you didn't see it, if you somehow managed to turn your eyes away from each new readout, someone was sure to mention it to you.

O'Niel looked up from the console he'd been processing paperwork on to stare out into the squad room. Two deputies had ceased running down a list of checkpoints that needed to be inspected that afternoon. Their attention was on the wall readout which calmly announced: SHUTTLE — IN TRANSIT. ARRIVAL 69 HOURS 56 MINUTES.

They looked at each other, muttered something, then glanced toward the office. When they saw O'Niel staring out toward them they hurriedly returned to their work. So did O'Niel, albeit more slowly.

It was night again in the Club. Within the transparent, floating cylinders a new pair of dancers undulated to the beat of fresh music, bathed in hot lights and their own sweat. The crowd milling around the bar and tables was as thick and boisterous as ever.

O'Niel walked in, spent a minute surveying the crowd before starting toward the bar. A few patrons near the entrance noticed him, began to converse in low tones. The comments spread. His presence was like a rock dropped in a pond. Ripples of conversation spread out in all directions from the common center of O'Niel.

The noise dimmed noticeably. All eyes were on him, staring at something extraordinary. The impact would have been less had a three-headed giraffe suddenly ambled into the Club and demanded a gin and tonic.

O'Niel acted as though nothing out of the ordinary was happening. He sauntered over to the bar, the men and women packed in front of him parting as neatly as ice before a hot wire.

He leaned over the bartop and stared at the tender.

"What'll you have, Marshal?" the man finally asked.

"Beer. House." He smiled thinly.

The bartender nodded, turned, and drew a glassful from a gleaming spigot.

O'Niel accepted the glass, lifted it to his lips, then hesitated. Everyone was still staring at him. He smiled inwardly. It was a silent toast, of a sort. He started in on the beer, ignoring the stares.

Gradually it dawned on the crowd that nothing exceptional was about to happen. In twos and threes they resumed their conversations. The men standing on either side of O'Neil picked up the broken threads of former arguments. Women workers chatted amiably with each other or their male counterparts.

But the intensity was down. Everyone sounded and acted slightly self-conscious. From time to time this man or that woman would glance over a shoulder to see if the Marshal happened to be staring at them.

He wasn't. His attention was on the steadily ticking readout glowing greenly on the far wall.

There were several deputies hard at work in the squad room. Ballard was behind the sergeant's desk, studying dispatches from the previous day, making a note here and there on acrylic boards, going over the assignments for the evening patrol.

After an hour or so of such paperwork the new sergeant found himself feeling itchy. He looked up and over at O'Niel's office to discover the Marshal staring directly at him through the glass partition. O'Niel motioned to him.

Ballard nodded, arranged his work neatly on the desk. He rose and moved into the Marshal's office.

"Yes, Sir?"

"Sit down, Sergeant." O'Niel was puffing on a cigarette as he motioned him to a chair.

Ballard sat. O'Niel put his feet up on his desk and did nothing. Just sat there, staring at the ceiling and puffing on the butt. Eventually he finished, discarded the stubble.

Ballard suspected what was coming. O'Niel was just taking his time getting around to asking the inevitable.

"How many can I count on?"

Ballard shifted uncomfortably in his chair, wishing he was somewhere else. "I . . . I don't know, Sir. It's a difficult situation."

O'Niel crossed one leg over the other and continued to regard the ceiling. It was an interesting mosaic of grid work and exposed conduits. He studied the patterns a while longer, spoke without looking at the man seated across from him.

"What about you?"

Ballard said nothing. After awhile O'Niel's gaze dropped, locked on the sergeant.

"Most of us," Ballard said hurriedly, "most are . . . we're young. We have families."

"I have a family," O'Niel quietly reminded him.

"I know, Sir. Except your family is . . . ." He broke off at the expression on the Marshal's face. "I'm sorry, Sir."

"That's okay." For a moment O'Niel's gaze was elsewhere. Then he was staring unaccusingly back at the sergeant. "It's true." There was another pause. Ballard was the best of the bunch, the biggest, and maybe the toughest. That was why he'd made him sergeant after Montone. Of all the deputies only Ballard didn't seem to tremble every time Sheppard's name was mentioned.

But if he wouldn't stand up now, then O'Niel knew the rest were useless. His tone changed to one of curiosity as he watched the sergeant.

"Tell me something. Think about it a minute. Do you," he gestured toward the half-filled squad room where arriving deputies were filing in, chatting and joking with each other, "do any of you care if the bad guys win?"

Whatever Ballard's reactions were he didn't ... or couldn't ... voice them. He looked away and said nothing, keeping his eyes on the floor. O'Niel found himself nodding slowly.

"Well ... at least we all know where we stand. Thank you, Sergeant. You can return to your regular duties. You have a shift roster to announce. That will be all."

Ballard rose, mumbled something incoherent as he retreated from the office. His eyes never rose to meet O'Niel's and he forgot to salute.

Out in the squad room he moved quickly to his desk and picked up the acrylic announcement board. Then he was reading out the posts for the next shift. The deputies listened attentively. There were none of the usual moans or wisecracks about individual assignments.

Most of the deputies kept their attention resolutely on the droning Ballard. A few found theirs' drawn to the steadily changing readout high up on the far wall. One or two sneaked hurried glances at the Marshal's office.

All were relieved when the last assignment had been handed out and they were able to escape from the confines of the squad room . . . .

X

Morning arrived weak but welcome. Distant sunlight outlined the mountains and sulfurous volcanoes, throwing the skeletal framework of the mine complex into sharp relief. Photons fell on the high-efficiency solar collectors. Generators began to hum, drawing and storing power.

On the wall above the shuttle dock access hatch a readout announced silently: SHUTTLE — IN TRANSIT. ARRIVAL — 40 HOURS 18 MINUTES.

O'Niel was alone in the white canyon of the court. He bounced the ball against the floor. The sound of it ricocheting off the hard wall accentuated his isolation. He slammed it back, held up his racket to backhand the return, and

managed to miss it. His swing, listless and indifferent, allowed the ball to bounce past him.

It rolled to the back end of the court, dribbled off into a corner. He watched it, making
no attempt to retrieve it even after it came to a
stop.

"That's pretty good," observed a sharp voice.
"Playing by yourself and losing. That takes a
considerable amount of concentration."

Lazarus closed the court entryway behind
her and strolled out onto the floor. O'Niel
didn't acknowledge her presence, didn't turn to
look at her.

She stopped and studied him, her forehead
wrinkling. "Looks like you'd benefit by a partner." She smiled hesitantly and gestured toward the ball. "I'd join you in this dumb game,
if I could play sitting down."

Whereupon she chose a relatively clean section of floor and sat down, crossing her legs as
she did so. O'Niel walked past her to retrieve
the ball. She watched him return to the serve
mark and stand there, considering his next
move.

"I've been well, thank you," she said in response to the unasked question. "Pretty busy,
too. Seems like there's some kind of flu going
around. That's a mighty rare occurrence in this
canned atmosphere because the samplers are
supposed to constantly monitor the junk and
suck out any dangerous germs or impurities.
But I guess some kind of bug's finally managed
to slip past them." She paused a moment. Still
O'Niel didn't speak, but he didn't serve the
ball, either.

"You have no idea how many workers are going to be sick by Sunday," she continued in mock amazement. "Extraordinary symptoms. Nothing like them in my reference library." She shifted her backside on the hard floor.

"No fevers, no stuffy noses, no aches and pains. Lots of eye trouble though. People seem unable to control their ocular muscles. They're able to look every which way except straight at you.

"There's also a lot of shortness of breath and heightened coloring, followed by a frantic desire to leave the infirmary once the disease has been recorded. Oh yes, lots of weakness-in-the-knees, too. Sometimes runs all the way up the spine." She scratched at her forehead, grinned humorlessly up at O'Niel.

"Yeah, it's your regular epidemic. First one I've run up against here on Io. No one seems immune. I've never seen anything spread so fast."

O'Niel used one shoe to rub at a scuff mark disgracing the highly polished floor. The scuff mark wouldn't come out but he kept at it as he spoke.

"What about you? Are you going to be sick this Sunday?"

Lazarus sucked in a deep breath, let the air out in a single whoosh. When she resumed talking the words came out in a flood. It was as if O'Niel had somehow turned a key inside her.

"You know, I was married once. I know that's hard to believe, but I was. A terrific guy. Gorgeous. Smart, clean, witty, just rakish enough in his personal likes and dislikes to keep you from getting bored.

"Eight years. We were really happy for about four, neutral for the next two, and genuinely miserable for the last couple." Her gaze rose to the ceiling and she stared reminiscently at the white enameled sky.

"I remember when we decided to get a divorce. It was a Saturday. The weather was beautiful. We went to a party. Really interesting people were there, which was unusual enough. Generally I hated parties. Still do, but this one was different, this one was decent.

"We had drinks and a fabulous dinner. Even the dessert was good. He looked over at me and I looked at him and we both knew it was over. Over cognac." She tried to smile but couldn't. "Our marriage was civilized, but over.

"He said, 'You know, I will always love you. I want you always to be happy. I hope you find someone else.'" She laughed lightly in remembrance.

"Class. That guy had what it takes in all departments, let me tell you. When you really care for somebody, you want them to be happy." She traced an invisible design on the floor.

"I looked back at him, smiled, and said, 'I hope you're miserable, and I hope your nose falls right off your face! Then I got drunk."

"Does all that have a point?" O'Niel eventually inquired gently.

"Sure it does. You think I'm just wasting air? You see, if I really had what it takes, I would have said the right thing. If I really had what it takes, I would never have wound up in this god-forsaken place. I'd be working on Luna, off-Earth but in luxury.

"What I'm trying to say is that if you're looking for sterling character you're in the wrong place. I don't qualify." He didn't say anything.

She leaned forward, spoke earnestly. "Listen, if you're the kind of man you're supposed to be you wouldn't stick around either. That's why they sent you here."

O'Niel said softly, "They made a mistake."

Lazarus shook her head again, her voice full of disappointment. "I was afraid you'd say something like that." She tried to peer beyond the quiet mask, past the beard and the dark eyes, but she couldn't find it, couldn't see what was driving him.

"You think you're making a difference by doing what you're doing here?"

He shrugged, bounced the ball a couple of times and considered the wall.

"Then why, for God's sake?"

O'Niel hesitated, then looked over at her. His whole manner was solemn. "Because maybe they're right. They sent me here to this pile of shit because they think I belong here. I've got to find out if they're right." He stopped bouncing the ball. When he spoke again there was more emotion in his face than she'd thought possible.

"Lazarus, there's a whole machine, a whole rotten stinking machine that works only because everybody connected with it does what they're supposed to. I found out I'm supposed to be a part of that. I'm supposed to be something I don't like. That's what it says in the program. That's my rotten little part in the rotten machine." He caught his breath, looked away.

"Well I don't like it. I don't like the machine and I don't like the part I'm supposed to play in it. So I'm going to find out if they're right." He turned on her.

"What do you think of that?"

She stared appraisingly back at him. "I think your wife is one stupid lady."

O'Niel tried to smile but only made it halfway. It was a triumph, of sorts.

"You want to go get drunk?" she asked him. She pointed at the racket. "Or you want to stay here and beat the hell out of a rubber ball?"

He didn't hesitate and tossed the racket and ball into a corner.

She struggled to her feet and headed for the exit, feeling good without really knowing why.

"At least you still have *some* sense left."

"Is that your professional opinion, doctor?"

"Are you kidding?" She broke into a twisted grin. "Professionally, you're mad as a March Hare. The other opinion, that's personal."

"Personally," he said as they left the court, "I tend to agree with the first . . . ."

Time passed slowly at the mine. It was as if someone had jimmied the clocks. They continued their relentless march toward tomorrows, but the minutes now seemed like hours, the seconds stretched into minutes.

The jokes and complaints and arguments the miners indulged in acquired a forced air. Once in a while some wit would venture a joke about the cause of the strain, get pained or angry looks instead of the expected laughs, and slink quietly back to work.

It wasn't just the miners. Everyone in the mine was on edge, from Admin down to Sanitation. There was a charge in the atmosphere that didn't come from a leak in the storage batteries.

When the Marshal walked through a crowded area, the tension fairly crackled.

Off in the distance on the western horizon an enormous volcano, a dark yellowish growth, suddenly became active. It heaved a blue white cloud into the black sky. There was a momentary crack in the psychological web that had enveloped the mine as this new concern took precedence.

Seismologists checked to make sure the tectonic activity was localized and that it presented no danger to the mine or its inhabitants. Everyone took time to watch the distant, silent eruption, the newcomers nervous, the old-timers lazily leaning against the quivering mine scaffolding or catching a quick nap inside their suits.

Though spectacularly violent, the eruption lasted only a few hours. Then Io's internal instability shifted and the activity moved a hundred miles southwestward. The all-clear sounded and everyone returned to work.

They were not particularly grateful for the respite. It was worse to stand around Outside with no work to do, more unsettling to consider Io's explosive innards, the nearness of space and the looming presence of Jupiter overhead than to grumble over a job. Work focused the mind and kept nervous threads of introspection from probing unpleasant regions.

For the next couple of days especially, it would be better not to do much thinking.

O'Niel tried to do the same, but there were no breaks in his routine to take his mind off the inexorable countdown of the clocks.

If anything, there was less trouble than normal. Fewer drunks and almost no fights. For whatever reasons it was as if there was an unspoken conspiracy among the workers not to cause trouble. Trouble would require the attention of the Marshal, and nobody wanted to make his acquaintance just then.

Involuntarily, O'Niel found himself looking up from his desk, out across the squad room at the readout set in the opposite wall. SHUTTLE — IN TRANSIT it read. ARRIVAL — 22 HOURS 15 MINUTES.

He reminded himself that he wasn't going to do that anymore. Irritated, he bent back to his work.

There were compartments to inspect, lockseals to check, small complaints to be processed and minor arrests to make out reports on. Each passed a little more time, caused it to slump forward a little faster. He checked out every surveillance camera in the complex personally, and then did it a second time. He filed reports and scanned personnel files, looking for clues to the identities of those coming to do Sheppard's dirty work.

But no matter how hard he tried, no matter

how assiduously he buried himself in busy-work, he still found himself glancing from time to time at the nearest readout.

It was the end of another shift and the deputies were filing out of the squad room. O'Niel sat at his desk, ignoring their by now open stares. He was eating a sandwich that had been left sitting too long. It had a consistency flattering to a fencepost, not digestion. The sawdust taste carried the analogy still further.

He rubbed his eyes and stared at the computer readout. All the names were running together, an endless chain of imponderables. The list was drawn from the personnel files of Station Green. Somewhere on the list was the name of one professional hitperson, probably more.

He didn't really expect to identify them by scanning the lists. A professional assassin would carry professional cover. But it was something to do.

Nuts. The names had melted into a single blur. It was time to rest, whether his brain wanted to or not. His body insisted.

The digital readout in his apartment was flashing steadily as he entered and turned on the lights. SHUTTLE — IN TRANSIT. AR-RIVAL — 9 HOURS 37 MINUTES.

Long day, long hours. He was so damn tired and the room was so empty. It was so quiet he could hear the couch fabric squeak when he sat down.

The beeping of the communicator was the last thing he expected to hear. A red light started flashing above the monitor. In the room's silence the erratic sound was startlingly loud.

It paralyzed him for a moment. The call was on his personal line, not the one linking his quarters to the office.

If he didn't move himself he'd never find out who it was. He stood, hurried to the console, and acknowledged the call.

The screen cleared, displaying large letters. O'NIEL, W.T. TELECOMMUNICATION — STATION GREEN — REAL TIME TRANS-MISSION.

He stared at the letters as though at any moment they might band together snake-like to jump out and bite him. Automatically his hand went to the top of the console to adjust the tiny video pickup positioned there, to make certain it was pointing at him. The pencil-sized camera hummed as its innards came alive.

He sat down, typed into the console O'NIEL, W.T. together with his personal code, then, PROCEED.

The letters vanished and were replaced with bright wavy lines indicative of momentarily confused electronics. The lines cleared, straightened, and he found himself staring at Carol. She looked back at him. He knew his own pickup must be working because she hurried to replace her look of concern with a smile.

"Hello there."

For a long moment he didn't reply, just stared at her, drinking in the vision. Her face was less haggard than it had been the last time he'd looked at it, via the taped message she'd left him. When she'd left him.

Don't think about that now, he commanded himself. There's not enough time left to waste any on that. Think about how beautiful she is, how warm and friendly-familiar. Not how far away.

"Hello there yourself." He summoned up a slight grin. It was very hard.

It flustered Carol. "I'm doing it again," she murmured unhappily. "I've had plenty of time to prepare what I was going to say. I was going to be so devastatingly clever. And here I am, looking at your face, and my mouth has gone to mush. Jesus."

"How is Paulie?" he asked.

She tried to regain her composure. "He's fine. I promised him he could talk to you." She gestured to her right. "He's in the next room, out of pickup range. Probably destroying the furniture."

Her voice trailed away, leaving an awkward silence. It made little difference to O'Niel. He was quite content just to look at her.

"Are you feeling well?" she finally asked. Anything but that torturous silence!

"I'm okay," he lied.

"I'm . . . ah, Paulie and I . . . our reservations have come through. We're booked on a flight home." O'Niel just nodded. She looked down, making a pretense of checking the console readouts at her end. "The reservations . . . I didn't think it would hurt . . . are for three."

O'Niel scrounged a cigarette from a console drawer, struck the end against the metal to light it. "That was very thoughtful of you."

"Please . . . ."

He cut her off quickly with a short, nervous

shake of his head, not wanting it to go on. "I can't."

She stared back at him, not understanding. "Why not, for God's sake?"

"I just can't." He wanted to look at her and not look at her, hold her close and send her away. "I wish I could."

"What is so important?"

She was bringing it all down on him, all over again, and it seemed so unfair. They'd been through it all a dozen times before and there was no need to do it again. The knot in his belly was big enough now. It was pointless to try and explain yet again and make it worse.

Besides, he had other things to worry about. He wanted desperately to tell her about Sheppard, about his situation, about the significance of the steadily down-counting readouts. He couldn't. It would have been unfair. He loved her too much for that.

So he waved loosely at the pickup and said, "I'm too tired to go into it now, Carol. I just can't leave." He made a gesture of helplessness. "That's all."

"Maybe that's *all* for you, but it's not enough for me," she shot back, unwilling to let it drop. "What is it? Do you think you're making a difference?" It came out half question, half accusation. "Do you think you're making the Universe a better place? Do you think what you're doing is worth giving up your family for?"

O'Niel tried to frame an answer, failed. In all the time they'd been married he'd never been able to compose a satisfactory one. He simply stared back at her, tired and sad-eyed.

She'd seen that look before, sighed resignedly. "You're a stubborn son-of-a-bitch."

"Yes," he agreed.

There was a pause. Then she must have seen something else in his face. Her voice changed and her expression turned wary.

"Something is wrong there, isn't it? Something serious that you're not telling me."

"No."

"You're in trouble. I know it. Every time you start speaking in sentences of less than two words I know you're in some kind of trouble."

He looked straight at her, forced himself to sound reassuring. "I'm okay."

She stared back at him, spoke through clenched teeth, the frustration nearly overwhelming her. "Damn you." Then she looked away from the pickup and called out, "Paulie! You can come in now." She faced him again, lowering her voice but not the intensity in it.

"I love you."

As she stepped aside an eager young face replaced hers. It lit up the screen, radiated happiness and innocence; two things O'Niel hadn't seen much of lately.

"Daddy!"

The knife floating in O'Niel's guts twisted. He fought to conceal the pain. "Hey, Paul. Good to see you. How are you doing?"

"Great. Mommy let me stay up late because this was when the call went through. They told us the lines Outland are always busy." He lost some of his initial enthusiasm. "I miss you."

"I miss you, too." The knife moved with exquisite delicacy.

"Mommy says as soon as you get done what you have to do, you're going to come home with us."

"As soon as I get done."

"What's it like on Earth?"

"It's beautiful." It had been a long time but O'Niel didn't have any trouble remembering. "You'll see so many wonderful things and have so many friends to play with. It'll be great."

"Mommy says on the flight they put you to sleep for a long time."

"For a while," he replied. "It won't seem like very long."

"Will it hurt?"

"Not even a little. It's just like going to sleep in your own bed. You'll just wake up and be home."

He looked doubtful. "I'm going to sleep through my birthday, mommy told me. How can I have a cake and a party if I'm sleeping?"

O'Niel smiled. "Next birthday you'll have a double party, and you'll get twice as many presents."

"Can't you come with us?"

"Not right now."

"Soon?"

"Yes . . . soon."

"I love you, Daddy."

That almost did it. A child's guileless plea can crumble even an iron will. O'Niel found himself choking on his next words, struggled to keep control of himself and the fatherly smile frozen in place.

"I . . . I love you, Paul. You take care of mommy now, until I can join you."

"I will. See you, Daddy."

The screen image broke apart, became a cluster of weaving, dancing lines. It looks like I feel, he thought glumly. He wasn't surprised Carol hadn't come back on. She'd already taken her best shot.

The screen patiently declared END TRANS-MISSION. O'Niel didn't deactivate it, kept staring at the words, replaying the whole transmission over and over in his mind's eye. It was quite a while before he turned it off. When he finally did so, the conversation had faded until it was just another hopeful dream.

It was busier than usual in the shuttle loading bay. The level of activity had been increasing for several hours. Landing crews bustled about checking their equipment and instrumentation, some real work soon to be required of them. Maintenance workers assisted in the ready-up. Huge containers of ore were given a final aligning while thick-soled convoyers were freshly lubricated and warmed up.

SHUTTLE — IN TRANSIT, the oversized readout shouted above the busy crews. ARRIV-AL — 1 HOUR 55 MINUTES.

The clip was plastic and so were the shells. The riot gun was designed to supply high stopping power at short range. A gauge and dial on the side allowed the user to adjust the velocity of each shell by modifying the solid shaped charge of propellant within. That way the wielder could do real damage to an assailant without blowing a hole through the vacuum-sealed corridors or accessways.

The empty clips were stacked next to a framed picture of Carol and Paul on the coffee table in O'Niel's apartment. A box of shells sat nearby.

O'Niel paused a moment to study the picture, noting that for once Paul's hair was neatly combed. Carol looked radiant.

Then he returned to loading shells into clips, his manner wholly businesslike. He positioned each shell as though his life might depend on its not jamming.

When he was finished he turned his attention to the gun which lay in pieces on the far end of the table. He checked each section before snapping it into place, adding a drop of oil here, blowing away a speck of lint there. The barrels were spotless, the firing mechanism free-flowing, the stock set firmly in place. He rechecked the lenses on the short sight, aimed the gun, and swung it from right to left.

He frowned and set the gun gently on the table. Using a tiny tool he adjusted the sliding weight set in the underside of the stock, moving it a millimeter rearward. Raising the weapon once more he went through the aiming procedure again, letting the gun balance in one hand. That was better.

Rising, he reached for the loaded clips piled alongside the picture and began slipping them into his pockets. The last thing he did before leaving the room was slide a full magazine into the gun.

The volume of sound issuing from the Club indicated that it held a fairly good-sized crowd. Music seeped out around the edges of the hatchway. The dancers would be off-duty now, O'Niel thought as he made his way through the accessway nexus. If he'd taken the time to peer inside he would have noticed that there was not a lot of mixing taking place but that the bar was exceptionally busy.

Sheppard was finishing his coffee ... real coffee ... and a breakfast of scrambled eggs and bacon. He glanced up at the neat digital readout imbedded in his desk monitor. It said in soft green: SHUTTLE — IN TRANSIT. ARRIVAL — 1 HOUR 32 MINUTES.

The bacon was properly cooked this morning. Crisp and not soggy. He used a piece of bread to shovel up the last of the scrambled eggs.

The corridor O'Niel had chosen was empty when he entered it. He'd checked out the previous one and hadn't encountered a soul.

Now he made his way casually down the little-used accessway. No one came up from behind to pass him and the hatch at the far end stayed shut.

Moving quickly he turned and unlatched the security panel hidden in the west wall, slipped the gun inside and locked the compartment. Then he continued on his way, taking a different path back to the office.

Activity in the shuttle loading bay increased. The landing crew was completing pressure tests on the lock, to ensure that no precious atmosphere would leak out while loading was in progress. Seals were triple-checked. The arrival of the shuttle was an ordinary occurrence that was always handled with extraordinary care.

It was crowded in the Admin Ward Room. Breakfast was still being served. Huge plates of fried, scrambled, and soft boiled eggs were interspersed on the tables with bowls of biscuits, gravy, grits, cereal, bacon, and muffins. There were cold flagons of several kinds of fruit juice, pitchers of milk, self-warming tanks of coffee and tea. The napkins were false linen instead of just paper.

As opposed to the frenetic blare of conversation in the workers' cafeteria the talk in the ward room was subdued. Its occupants preferred to affect a genteel air they had not been born to. It gave the Sunday brunch the feel of a gathering at some Earthside Country Club.

Soft lighting made the imported food look even better than it was. The women sometimes moved to form their own bubbly, animated groups while the men would sit swapping jokes or production figures or, in a more serious vein, this or that problem at the mine.

They managed the admirable task of ignoring the one problem that was on everyone's mind.

Above the tables and conversation the room readout flashed: SHUTTLE — IN TRANSIT. ARRIVAL — 0 HOURS 43 MINUTES. No one paid it any attention. It was only a clock. Shuttles arrived every week, on schedule.

O'Niel strode through the front entrance and looked around. Sheppard was not present. The General Manager often preferred to eat in the privacy of his own office and this morning was no exception.

It was several seconds before the Marshal's presence was noticed. As soon as it was the conversation faded faster than a liter of oxygen exposed on Io's surface. Everyone turned to look at him.

He stood in the doorway and smiled pleasantly back at them.

Within the shuttle bay a pulsating horn began to wail. Lights flashed and startled attendants rushed to man their positions. There were a number of muffled curses as coffee was hastily downed or abandoned. The readout overhead flashed: SHUTTLE — OUTER MARKER. ARRIVAL — EARLY.

O'Niel studied the silent group of diners, said conversationally, "Good morning."

A few subdued "good mornings" drifted up to him. Hands fumbled with glasses and utensils but no one resumed eating. O'Niel started toward the nearest table, mentally noting who was present and who was not.

He recognized one face, shifting toward her. She tried to smile back at him.

"How are you, Ms. Spector?"

The woman who'd greeted him so warmly his first official day at the mine looked flustered. "Uh, fine, thank you, Marshal." She almost started to ask reflexively, "How are you," but caught herself in time.

O'Niel turned his attention to her breakfast companion. "Mr. Rudolph? You doing okay this morning?"

"Morning, Marshal. I'm fine, yes." Rudolph stirred his hot cereal nervously.

O'Niel's gaze rose. He scanned the room, locking eyes with those not looking elsewhere.

"I hope everyone's fine this morning. I hope you're all having a pleasant time." He walked past one of the serving tables. "Looks good." He selected an apple from one plate, began gnawing on it. The sound was loud in the suddenly silent room.

In the shuttle bay access hatches slammed shut. There was a tremendous, steady hiss as the main airlock was readied for pressurization. The ground crews strained with their heavy equipment. Loaders stood by, idling smoothly as they waited to stuff the incoming ship's cargo hold with containers of dark ore.

High above, the station landing tower operators monitored their consoles and ignored distant volcanic upheavals. Jupiter glowered overhead, a claustrophobic orange presence. Readouts gave constant readings of fluctuations in the giant planet's powerful magnetic field, radiation belts and outer atmosphere. Others changed steadily as a graphic outline grew larger on the main screen.

High above a pair of intensely bright white lights appeared. As the shuttle came nearer the white spots became brilliant shafts of illumination directed downward. They lit up the yellowed surface of Io and flashed on the outer framework of the mine.

The shuttle was a boxy, massive gray construct, spotted here and there with official markings and unofficial dents and bruises. It was not streamlined and would never enter any atmosphere denser than Io's.

Great pylons joined cylindrical compartments the size of buildings: the ship's cargo holds. Near the front of the vessel were inter-locked geometric shapes that held crew and passengers.

Engines fired silently in the near-emptiness above the mine as the vast, mobile transport shifted slightly to its left and continued to descend. Instructions traveled from the tower workers to the human pilots, then to the shuttle's computers. It adjusted speed and attitude accordingly, slowing as it neared the bay. The great clamshell doors were open to receive it.

O'Niel finished the apple, considered an English muffin, but decided against it. He stood in the middle of the room and regarded his colleagues.

"I don't mean to disturb you and I don't want anyone to get upset, but I could use a little help."

No one was rude enough to continue eating. The Administrative staff, the aristocracy of Io, was nothing if not polite. The variety of gestures and glances they individually employed to avoid looking back at the Marshal was impressive in its diversity.

O'Niel's expression never changed. "I thought so."

There was no comment, no response. A little more fidgiting, perhaps.

A breakfaster seated near the front of the room, a balding middle-aged computer specialist named Rudd, at least had the guts to stand up and say what most of them were thinking.

"You're supposed to protect us, Marshal. Not the other way around. It's your job, not ours. We do ours and you're supposed to do yours."

Mutters of support for this stance rose from indeterminate locations, emboldening the diminutive Rudd to continue.

"You're the police. I don't ask you to do my work. Why should I be expected to help you with yours? I have my own assistants. Where are your people?"

"My people?" O'Niel smiled pleasantly. "My people stink." He looked past Rudd as though the man wasn't there, at the others. "What about you good people?"

Nobody moved. Nobody replied.

O'Niel nodded once, dismissing them. "Enjoy your breakfast." He turned and walked out . . . .

XI

Forward engines fired, slowing the giant shuttle craft further. The crews waiting inside the loading bay could feel the nearness of the ship as its engines' downblast sent a steady vibration through the entire complex.

Within the control tower orders were given in quiet, businesslike tones. Hydraulic access landing arms folded back, opening like a monstrous metal flower to receive the slowly descending vessel. Four maintenance gantries swung aside as blast deflector plates rose to shield the delicate framework of the tower and the rest of the mine.

Landing struts unfolded from the shuttle's belly as it hovered a few yards above the landing circle. It hung there on its repellers as the internal guidance computer matched readings with those in the tower and lined up with the sensors built into the structure of the landing platform.

Like the legs of a clumsy gray beetle the landing struts touched down against the receiving platform. Squinting against blinding landing lights the crews inside could now make out the ship through thick ports. The roar of the engine-induced internal vibrations was deafening inside the loading bay.

As the shuttle relaxed the landing struts collapsed into its underside. Recoil hydraulics and springs absorbed its weight which even in Io's light gravity was still considerable.

Tower operators acknowledged the successful touchdown. Within the shuttle cockpit its human pilots shut down engines and all other landing functions preparatory to commencing disembarkation procedures.

Landing lights dimmed. The maintenance gantries whirred back into position. Blast shields were withdrawn. Although the shuttle had barely touched down busy crews were already readying her for liftoff.

Vibration faded as the engines were shut down and conversation took its place inside the loading dock. Men and machines surged forward toward the ship. Huge metal arms hung ready to grasp off-loading cargo while lifters manipulating massive ore containers lined up to stuff the empty cargo holds full of pre-processed Ilmenite.

The readout above the dock had ceased blinking. SHUTTLE — DOCKED it shone steadily. OFF LOADING IN PROGRESS.

O'Niel arrived at the squad room on the run. The readout on the far wall confirmed what he'd been told. Why the shuttle had arrived an unannounced half hour early was a question he dearly wished the answer to, but there was no time for casual inquiries now. It was doubtful the shuttle pilots themselves could give him a reasonable explanation. The origin of their orders would probably have been effectively obscured.

He grabbed the other riot gun from its rack and stuffed extra clips into his pockets. A glance showed him what he had expected: Security was deserted.

Throwing himself into the seat before the computer console in his office he hurriedly keyed in a request, marked it urgent.

O'NIEL, W.T. REQUEST LIKENESS OF PERSONNEL ON PASSENGER MANIFEST ON PRESENT SHUTTLE WHO WERE TICKETED WITHIN THREE DAYS OF DEPARTURE. CROSS REFERENCE WITH PERSONNEL ON MANIFEST WITH PRIOR ARREST RECORD.

The machine hummed, responded with its usual speed. The response, however, was not what he expected.

NEGATIVE DATA AVAILABLE.

The past several days had given O'Niel plenty of time to think. Sometimes he'd felt sorry for himself. Now and then he wondered if perhaps he hadn't made the wrong decision. Often he'd been worried. He'd invented any number of possible scenarios for what might happen subsequent to the shuttle's arrival. Some of them had bordered on the bizarre, others on the fanciful. Not a few had been awash in wish fulfillment.

But this was the first time he'd been confused.

Computers did not confuse, they elucidated. The intricate and efficient advanced security machinery was the one thing he'd always been able to depend upon, no matter where he'd been stationed. It couldn't run out on him like his deputies or beg off with rationalizations like those faceless, gutless citizens whose breakfast he'd interrupted.

The one ally he hadn't expected to betray him was his computer.

For several minutes he simply sat and stared at it. Unlike Ballard, it didn't turn away from him. But Ballard's reaction he could understand. The computer's baffled him.

Try again, he told himself. You can afford to give up anything but time.

His fingers moved with deliberate precision over the keyboard. O'NIEL, W.T. PREVIOUS REQUEST MADE WITH SECURITY PRIORITY — REPLY.

NEGATIVE DATA AVAILABLE, the machine silently insisted.

Take it easy, he ordered himself. Think it through. The machine wasn't lying to him, therefore its demoralizing response must be grounded in fact. Question the question, not the reply.

He forced himself to remain calm as he inquired again. O'NIEL, W.T. EMERGENCY SECURITY REQUEST FOR DATA. WHY NEGATIVE RESPONSE?

Letters flashed promptly on the screen. NO MANIFEST TRANSMITTED FROM STATION—SHUTTLE DEPARTURE POINT.

Now that he could understand, if not enjoy. O'NIEL, W.T. he typed in. URGENT REQUEST FROM IO SECURITY TO STATION GREEN TO TRANSMIT REQUESTED DATA IMMEDIATELY.

NEGATIVE ABILITY, came the maddening response. VOICE AND PICTURE TRANSMISSIONS WITH STATION GREEN — SHUTTLE DEPARTURE POINT TEMPORARILY TERMINATED.

REASON FOR TERMINATION? he asked.

NEGATIVE DATA AVAILABLE.

He sat back in the chair and stared dazedly at the bank of monitors. Without positive replies to his questions, without the computer's assistance, he at one stroke lost the aid of a hundred fifty years of law enforcement advances. A single well thought-out countermove had thrown him back to purely primitive methods.

No, that wasn't entirely true. He wasn't down to sticks and stones yet. Ignoring the ineffective trans-spatial monitor he turned his attention to the local cluster of surveillance screens.

The shuttle loading dock appeared on one. He touched additional controls. At least he wasn't completely blind. Another screen revealed the glowing corridor of the main passenger access tube, other screens the passageways and tunnels spreading outward from the bay.

The passenger elevator had already started

down its service gantry, carrying the new arrivals. Inside the bay the landing crews busied themselves at various tasks. A rich hiss issued from the dock monitor.

A lighted display above the main access corridor announced ACCESSWAY — ZERO ATMOSPHERE. Seconds passed and it changed to ACCESSWAY — PRESSURIZING and at last to ACCESSWAY — FULL ATMOSPHERE AND GRAVITY.

The hissing faded and the hatchway sealing the bayside end of the tube was opened. The passengers were still out of sight, having just left the transporting elevator at the far end of the corridor. Members of the landing crew stood lazily around the open hatch, occasionally checking readouts but mostly looking bored.

O'Niel sat in the empty office and watched the open end of the tube attentively. He was anything but bored. Soon shadows appeared, lit by the lights at the far end of the tube. Then men and women appeared.

Some chatted animatedly, others were silent, still others looked curiously about with attitudes varying from those approaching purgatory to travelers simply returning to a familiar place. All carried nylon duffle bags of varying colors. Most of the talking ceased when they reached the end of the corridor and stepped out into the dust-filled loading bay.

O'Niel stared at the screen showing the arrivals. He scrutinized each debarking man and woman closely, trying to pick out the assassins among them. But whoever they were they remained unidentifiable. As the transmission he'd intercepted had indicated, they were professionals. It would take more than appearance to separate them from their non-lethal brethren.

There were twenty passengers altogether. Processing was brief and casual. Ticket records were checked against faces, destinations within the mine noted, directions provided by the landing crew and that was all. The newcomers were sent on their way. There was no reason for more elaborate rituals. No one had any reason to want to smuggle themself onto Io.

The twenty crossed the open landing bay and entered a white corridor, the main accessway to the rest of the mine. At its terminus was a hexagonal junction from which five sub-corridors led to the five major sections of the complex. O'Niel touched controls, switched screens to jump ahead of the arrivals. The new picture gave him a clear view of the multiple junction.

As the passengers entered the terminus they split into smaller groups, a few taking each sub-corridor. Some said good-byes to friends made on shipboard while others resumed former conversations.

Eventually the last two men arrived at the junction. They were chatting easily and in appearance were no different from any of the other passengers. If anything, they were excessively ordinary-looking.

After another minute or two of discussion they suddenly lapsed into silence and executed a thoroughly un-ordinary inspection of the six corridors. Apparently satisfied they set their duffle bags down on the junction floor and unsealed them.

Buried among clothing, personal effects, and toiletries were bits of metal which were extricated one at a time, each piece fitting into the one that had preceded it. The men alternated assembling, one snapping a folding stock into a barrel while his companion maintained a watch on the corridors. Then he would affix sight and barrel while the other kept watch.

They worked smoothly and in tandem, building and watching, trigger mechanisms and guards, lastly straps and loaded magazines.

Weapons completed, each man hefted his duffle bag and started off down a different corridor. Not a word had been spoken since they'd commenced assembling the guns, not a word was offered in departure.

O'Niel studied them intently as they split, recording the directions they took. They both walked at the same pace: steadily, deliberately but without wasting time. He shifted cameras to keep ahead of them.

It was hard to say for certain but the first man seemed to be taking the more direct path to Administration. When they finished there they would likely continue on their separate ways before linking up outside Security. Waiting to confront both of them together would be worse than foolish. The Marshal made a quick decision, hefted the riot gun, and hurried out of the office.

The Club was packed, the dancers in the midst of changing shifts. The transparent cylinders had been drawn up into the roof, where the change-over could be made in privacy. Professionals, the dancers were particular about their privacy. They didn't mind being looked at: that was what they were paid for. But there was nothing artistic about being groped. To the on-lookers in the Club the difference seemed small, to the dancers it defined the parameters of their profession.

The music raged in their absence, as did conversation and drinking. Much of the conversation was forced and the usual spontaneity was lacking. The same could have been said of the drinking.

Damned paperwork, Sheppard was thinking as he studied the figures glowing on his desk console. Fit duty for an administrative clerk, not a General Manager. Besides, it was taking time away from practising his chip shots.

He touched controls and figures on the screens shifted, changed. He was in a rush to finish off the morning's work. Behind him, cool greenery and a dimpled ball awaited.

The first gunman reached the men's locker room. He did not carry a map, having memorized the entire complex layout of the mine prior to setting foot on the shuttle. He glanced down at his wrist chronometer. As planned, the locker room was deserted, it being close to shift change-over. Night workers would just be making their way toward the elevators, the day shift filling their tanks prior to going Outside.

Starting from the far end he started working his way up one of the empty aisles.

His associate was climbing down a ladder to a lower passageway. He paused a moment, checking the schematic in his head before eventually turning to his right. Then it was down a long corridor, up another ladder and straight ahead.

Once he encountered two workers heading toward him. In a single smooth motion he slipped the gun inside the open duffle bag. They smiled at him as they passed and he returned the smile. The smile, vanishing as soon as they did, was replaced by the reappearance of the gun, tidy, compact, devoid of shine. The finish was purposely dull to keep it from reflecting light.

The man turned another corner, gripping the metal firmly. Like any craftsman he took care of his tools. No one else confronted him as he entered the Admin living quarters.

He began to move more carefully, especially when he turned up a certain corridor. No one emerged from behind any of the closed doors lining the corridor but he paid close attention to each of them all the same. Most of his attention was reserved for a door on his right, growing nearer with each step.

Flattening himself against the corridor wall he studied the door. The lockseal was on. Reaching into a jacket pocket he removed a tiny disc the size of a thumbnail. Crouching low he moved forward and touched the underside of the disc to the lockseal slit. There was no sound and the red warning light remained lit.

The man took a slow, deep breath and then swung his left leg around in a vicious kick. The door flew open and he shoved the muzzle of his gun inside. There was no reaction from beyond.

He edged around the opening, his finger tense on the trigger, and swept the apartment interior. Then he walked in, checked the computer station behind the couch, the chairs, even the corners of the ceilings to make certain nothing was hiding suspended in the shadows.

Cautiously he approached the door leading to O'Niel's bedroom, kicked it open. O'Niel was not present. He did the same with bathroom, then rechecked the apartment and lastly the closets.

He was disappointed. Shrugging, he turned and started for the next checkpoint.

O'Niel entered the worker's cafeteria. It was off-time for both staffs, at least an hour to the next meal. There was no one in sight.

The tables were clean and bare, the chairs empty and stacked on the tabletops. He'd never been in a completely empty cafeteria before. There was an eerie quality to it, as though the shades of the workers who ate there were hanging around after meals, swapping noncorporeal jokes in inaudible whispers.

He started through the tables, heading for the back exit. His attention was on the sealed door there.

There was an ear-busting roar and a bright

flash of orange that momentarily blinded him. The ceiling seemed to explode. Semi-automatic rounds of tracers fried the air around him as he went down and rolled, sparks flying from the ranked tables as the tracers and non-incendiary rounds screeched off their metal surfaces.

Silhouetted against the slits of light from the gridwork that formed the ceiling was the man with the gun. He was looking toward the floor, trying to track the rolling, twisting O'Niel while firing through an open lighting port.

O'Niel swung the riot gun around and blindly blazed away at the ceiling as he continued his mad tumble across the floor. He barely made it back to the front corridor ahead of the tracers that shattered behind him.

The Greenhouse was a good place to catch your breath. It boasted the freshest, sweetest-smelling air on Io. Rows of hydroponic platforms held burgeoning racks of fresh vegetables and fruits that flourished beneath long fluorescent tubes that put out consistent controlled wavelengths and continuously circulating, nutrient-heavy water that swirled around their roots.

Jupiter was a glowing threat in the sky above the glass dome. The distant star called Sol barely reached here and did not figure in the growing process. Automatics monitored the concentration of nutrients in the water, the burn time of the fluorescents, and even managed the pruning and cleanup.

They did not react to O'Niel's arrival. Checking the vast open space and seeing no hint of movement, he waited there, catching his wind.

A hand adjusted the monitors in the squad room. They showed O'Niel inside the Greenhouse. Others revealed the locations of the two gunmen. The hand moved away, left the screens burning. There was no one present in the squad room to see the main door close quietly.

O'Niel studied the open expanse of green and glass again. His gaze went upward, to the maintenance catwalk that ran through the branches of the fruit trees.

Turning, he opened a panel and traced circuitry until he found the switch he wanted. With a touch, the Greenhouse was plunged into darkness. The only light came from tiny tubes set into the floor gridwork.

He fumbled his way toward the ladder leading upward and started for the catwalk. As he reached up to grab the walkway railing the metal erupted in flame. The air hailed tracers and sparks showered off the tormented metal.

Blood spurted from his shoulder. He fell, the riot gun going one way, he another. Somehow he managed to spin, but instead of landing on his head he fell on the damaged shoulder, let out an involuntary grunt of pain.

Then he was up, holding his bleeding arm as he ran for the accessway.

In the darkness behind him a figure muttered angrily to itself. It loaded a fresh magazine into the squat weapon it held and swept the black dome with the starlight scope. Plants and floor showed up clearly in the lens, but this time there was nothing moving.

The man sighed, upset with his failure. He'd hurried the shot, promised himself firmly that he wouldn't make that mistake again. Dropping silently from the branches of the apple tree he'd been concealed in he loped off in pursuit of his bleeding quarry.

Gasping, O'Niel stumbled down the corridor. Repeated glances showed that it was still deserted behind him. It wouldn't stay that way for long. His shoulder was on fire.

He passed through a connecting hatchway and turned down yet another corridor. Still no shells whined through the air around him. He still had a chance.

There was the place in the wall. He touched the hidden buttons, waited. The panel swung open and he reached gratefully inside.

The backup gun he'd so carefully prepared wasn't there.

The instant of panic passed quickly, overwhelmed by the rush of time. He could die wondering what had happened to the other riot gun. Still holding his shoulder and fighting for breath he staggered on down the corridor.

It led him to a major junction. He stood in the center, blood trickling down his arm, trying to decide which way to run.

One of the hatch covers on his left started to whirr. There was someone on the other side, someone wanting in. He looked around desperately, but he was in the wrong place from which to make a quick escape.

No matter which corridor he chose he could only be halfway down it by the time whoever was on the other side of the opening hatch entered the juction. Every corridor was straight. He'd make an easy target in any of them.

All he could do was flatten himself against the wall next to the hatchway and hope that whoever it was behind it would be so anxious to run him down he wouldn't think to check behind him. He didn't hold out much hope for that. His hunters had already demonstrated their skill. But it was all he could think of to do.

The seals opened and the hatchcover swung outward. O'Niel readied himself for the inevitable, raised his good arm to strike at the man's neck as quickly as possible.

He stopped in mid-swing as the figure jumped fearfully out of the way. It was Lazarus.

"Jesus, O'Niel! Take it easy."

He stared dumbfoundedly at her, his own desperation temporarily forgotten. "What the hell are you doing here?"

"I'm a schmuck," she informed him. "I went to your office to see if I could help. I saw you on the surveillance screens. You ran out so fast you forgot to turn them off." She nodded back the way he'd come.

"You were headed right for one of them, you know."

He fingered his burning shoulder. "You're kidding me."

She didn't reply, cocked her head to one side as she gave the wound a cursory examination.

"You look in terrific shape. It looks messy

but they missed the artery. I'll stop the bleeding."

"How? I ran into the other one in the cafeteria. If he's working in tandem with the one in the Greenhouse, that would put him between us and the infirmary."

"Boy, are you indoctrinated. You think I'm helpless without my machines? This way."

She led him into the male worker's dormitory. They checked the aisles cautiously but the huge room was still empty. Lazarus went to an open bunk, cut part of a pillowcase, and began binding up his shoulder.

His attention was still on the front entrance, where they'd entered. "Did you see where they were heading? I'm just guessing. They should be planning to link up."

She spoke while concentrating on the bandage. "I think they were going for the operation wing. They're trying to cut you off from your office."

He nodded thoughtfully. "That's sensible, since they know now I'm not waiting for them there. Once they cut me off they'll start trying to back me into some nice empty section, like Hydroponics. Almost got me there once already." He paused, looked down at her.

"Start sealing off the accessways in the East Quadrant. I've got to get around them before they have a chance to catch me in a crossfire somewhere without witnesses."

"You really think types like that give a shit about witnesses, O'Niel?"

"If it came down to it they'd blow me away in the middle of the Club, but if they have a chance to do it unobserved, yeah, they'll work for it. Guys like that take pride in doing a clean job."

"How are you going to get around them? I watched them both on the monitors. They're checking everything down to the cracks in the floors."

"By going Outside."

The first gunman was taking his time. He was still anxious to be over with it, but he'd already rushed himself once and had no intention of doing so again. Patience was harder, but safer.

Besides, judging by the trail of blood O'Niel was leaving behind there was no need to rush.

Lazarus, continuing to work on the Marshal's injured shoulder, finished securing the bandage with a flourish. O'Niel inspected the result, moved the arm. It still hurt, but the pain no longer blinded him.

"Thanks."

"Don't misconstrue this," she warned him, looking anxiously toward the locker room entrance. "I'm not displaying character. Just temporary insanity."

Something made a noise at the end of the corridor leading toward the dormitory. O'Niel jumped up from the bunk. Lazarus froze.

Someone was coming down the corridor toward them. They could hear the footsteps on the metal floor. Of course, it might only be a worker trying to get an early start on his shift, but that was unlikely.

O'Niel gestured and Lazarus followed him.

They made their way past the darkened bunks, down one of the metal walkways into the assembly area. They waited there, hardly daring to breathe, until the footsteps and a hesitant shadow had passed on overhead.

O'Niel leaned down to Lazarus' level and kept his eyes on the top of the stairwell as he whispered to her. "I'm going Outside. Seal the doors like I told you to and get the hell out of this."

He moved to his right, studied the ranks of empty environment suits before selecting one approximating his size. Lazarus stood nearby, watching him.

O'Niel looked back at her and his voice rose slightly. "Go *on*."

"I can still help here," she whispered back.

The suit had been designed to be put on slowly and carefully. O'Niel struggled hastily into it. "Shit. Don't argue with me."

She was persistent. "I can help."

He stopped what he was doing, stared at her for a long moment. "All right. The access corridor between Buildings B and C."

She nodded understandingly. O'Niel finished donning the suit and hurried to the elevator airlock. As he waited for it he looked back toward her, seemed about to say something.

"Don't get maudlin," she warned him.

He didn't reply, turned away to face the rising elevator. The doors opened and he stepped in, sealing it behind him. The lift started upward with a soft whine.

Footsteps sounded on the level above. Lazarus flattened herself against the wall as the shadow passed over her a second time.

The elevator slowed, stopped as the lights for LEVEL ONE flashed on above the door. O'Niel pressed himself tight against the interior wall as the lift door slid aside, but the platform outside was empty.

He left the lift, moved carefully to the railing, and peered over the side. He was out of the range of artificial gravity and had to watch his stride lest he go soaring over the edge.

Mine scaffolding vanished down into the black depths of the crater, a descending framework of bright lights and steel. Building C was on his left and he started toward it, climbing up the exterior gridwork. The light gravity made it possible for him to float upward.

From the roof he could see the entire mine complex; the crater walls, the multiple buildings, even the shuttle dock. Jupiter filled the sky above the forest of lights and lacy gridwork. He forced himself not to look upward, assured his mind that Jupiter was not about to fall and crush him like a gnat. It was hard. He wasn't used to working Outside.

Moving lithely along the roof he came to the far side of the structure, looked down. A strand of plastic and metal linked Building C with Building B. The accessway was translucent and lit from within. O'Niel started inching his way down the side of the building toward it.

The first gunman was making his way slowly down yet another empty aisle. He passed close to Lazarus, who backed through the shower room toward the rear entrance. She didn't make a sound.

The hunter's senses were unusually acute, however. Even the soft brush of shoe against floor brought him up short. He held his breath, listening, the gun ready to swing in any direction.

Lazarus moved her foot again to make sure that he'd heard her, then broke for the access hatchway. She opened it, hurried into the corridor beyond, and opened the next hatch.

The gunman swept the light-gathering sight across the area, found nothing. That's when Lazarus chose to shut the hatch cover. She made certain it closed noisily.

It didn't provoke the gunman. He turned to look toward the source of the sound. Using the sight first he made his way through the shower area, then into the corridor.

Lazarus was running toward the far end of the accessway. She opened the hatch there, forced herself to stand and wait, her heart beating too fast.

O'Niel continued to make his way down the side of Building C. Only the light gravity made the awkward descent possible. Fortunately he didn't suffer from vertigo or even the gentle climb might have paralyzed him. There was a sheer drop of hundreds of feet only inches away.

He reached the edge of the roof, jumped carefully and landed on the top of the accessway linking the two major structures. For a second he almost overbalanced, but caught himself and started forward. Metal bands encircled the corridor, marking the places where the prefabricated sections of the tube were joined together.

Then he turned to look back toward Building C, and waited . . . .

XII

When the gunman entered the accessway the
first thing he saw was the figure at the far end.
It was distant and indistinct, but it reacted to
his appearance by frantically swinging wide
the hatchcover at the far end. The man reacted
in turn, touched the light trigger.

Lazarus jumped through the opening the
moment she saw the gunman appear, closing
the hatch just as he fired. Tracers rattled like
wasps off the metal, only slightly louder than
the pounding of her heart.

The noise didn't reach O'Niel, crouching
above on the top of the accessway, but he saw
the subdued sparkle of the tracers. Cursing the
clumsy pressurized suit he started to loosen the
emergency bolts that held the two sections of
corridor together.

The gunman had started down the access-way, and he was frowning inwardly. The figure which had fled from him seemed too small to be the Marshal. But it had reacted to him on sight. That implied some kind of connection with his designated target. Possibly the Marshal was with the smaller person and had preceded him through the hatch.

In that case the chase would end soon. What troubled the gunman was that he'd been assured the Marshal would have no help. He didn't like surprises. Not that it would make any difference in the end—an amateur ally or two wouldn't save O'Niel.

As to the problem of explaining two or more deaths instead of one, well, that wasn't his department. His wasn't the expository end of the business.

Two more, O'Niel thought nervously. Just another pair. He could see the silhouette of the gunman moving toward him in the corridor below. He'd better not look up, better concentrate on Lazarus. There was no way O'Niel could retreat to the safety of Building C in time if the gunman noticed him working above. He wouldn't be stupid enough to blaze away through the ceiling of the accessway, but a single small caliber shot wouldn't pose much risk and it could finish O'Niel.

Lazarus sealed the far hatch. Seconds later the alert hunter thought he saw something moving overhead. His frown deepened. At first he thought it might be the shuttle, but it was still too early for it to depart. No way it could have finished on-loading so soon.

Then he thought it must be some mainte-

nance worker busy at some routine task. Except
... there wasn't anything to maintain Outside.
An accessway carried no live conduits or piping—it was just a tunnel between structures.
What could the man be working on?

His gaze traveled to the far hatchway, now
tightly sealed ahead of him, then back to the
similarly closed barrier he'd just traversed.
There was no way he could reach either hatch
and open it in time.

He had just enough time to panic.

He raised his gun and started to reset the
velocity and charge. There was a faint hissing
sound. With an inarticulate cry he turned and
raced for the nearest hatch just as O'Niel unlatched the last bolt.

The two accessway sections separated a couple of inches. O'Niel fell backward as a thin
stream of red and white gushed out into space.
The white was frozen oxygen. The red was
what remained of the man who'd been trying
to kill him. He gripped the thin reinforcement
ridge running the length of the corridor to
keep from being blown off by the blast of escaping atmosphere. Killer and cloud dissipated
toward Jupiter.

Lazarus was leaning against the sealed
hatch. A red light was blinking on the door and
a readout was flashing angrily:

DANGER! CORRIDOR LEAK — NEGA-
TIVE ATMOSPHERE AND PRESSURE.
EMERGENCY LOCKSEAL IS NOW IN
PLACE. NOTIFY MAINTENANCE IMME-
DIATELY. NOTIFY MAINTENANCE IM-
MEDIATELY.

Maintenance would have to wait until she caught her breath, she thought exhaustedly. And perhaps longer than that.

Breakfast was proceding smoothly in the Administration Ward Room. Conversation had picked up from the previous day and appetites, the cooks noted, appeared to have improved. In the Club, business was brisk, liquor and propositions flowing freely.

O'Niel had left the unbolted corridor and made his way back to the top of Building C. He'd allowed himself five minutes to gain strength, had ingested as much of the liquid nutrients the suit carried as his stomach could stand. Nothing remained of the first gunman.

Lazarus reached the squad room, burst in and hurriedly checked the automatic surveillance monitors. They continued to function.

She hesitated over the unfamiliar bank of controls. The designations were different, but the system was similar enough to the medical monitors she used daily for her to give the instrumentation a try. She touched controls and buttons, trying to locate the second gunman.

O'Niel had gained the inspection catwalk that ran atop the building and was making his way back toward the Hydroponics station. If his guesses proved correct, the remaining gunman should be somewhere in the general area of the Greenhouse.

The second hunter was closer than that, having just entered the far end of glass dome. It was still dimly lit and he was using his scope to sweep the grounds.

Lazarus hadn't found him yet, continued fooling with the monitor instrumentation. A shadow suddenly fell on the screens. She whirled, eyes wide.

"Can I help?"

Not yet, heart, she told herself. It was deputy . . . now sergeant, she noted . . . Ballard. She relaxed, then found herself snapping at him.

"Terrific timing. Here comes the cavalry. You're a bit late, you know."

"Better late than never, right?" He was trying to see around her, peering anxiously toward the screens. "Is the Marshal all right?"

"So far. Shoulder wound, but it's not bad."

Ballard moved toward the monitors and she stepped aside. "Where is he now?"

Lazarus' frustration was clear in her voice. "Damned if I know. I've been hunting for him myself. He's Outside someplace."

Ballard frowned. "Outside? Where Outside?"

"How the hell should I know? I told you, I've been looking for him." She gestured at the console. "This is your toy, not mine. Maybe the Greenhouse. That's close by where he went out and there's another entry port near there."

O'Niel had spotted the second gunman, outlined against the gridwork lighting in the Greenhouse. Now he was making his cautious way up the glass side of the dome, crawling slowly so as not to attract the attention of the man with the gun.

His position was much more vulnerable than it had been atop the accessway. The roofing material here was transparent, not translucent. He'd make an easy target. Only the branches and leaves of the larger plants helped to conceal his presence.

His situation was the same in that the gunman could only fire a single shot or two at him. But this time he was the one without the margin of retreat. The gunman could move to the hatchway and stand next to it when he fired, instead of having to rush the length of a long corridor.

He continued making his way along the surface of the dome, heading toward the catwalk that crossed it lengthwise. There was a small platform at the apex full of repair material, and O'Niel had an idea.

Ballard studied the monitors, wished he had O'Niel's facility for operating the remote cameras. "So you think the Greenhouse?"

Lazarus turned to him uncertainly, a question poised on her lips. But he was already running from the squad room.

O'Niel paused to glance over the sheer side of the Greenhouse. The lower mine platforms were a field of tiny lights far below. They looked like small night-blooming flowers. Nearby were the enormous solar collectors, a rippling field of dark surfaces pointed toward the distant sun. They dwarfed the power plant they served.

Below him, the second gunman was slowly making his way through the dome.

Ballard reached the small elevator bay and found an atmosphere suit. It wasn't his but it fitted reasonably well. He started to struggle into it.

O'Niel reached the catwalk platform, climbed onto it. The catwalk was a length of spider silk strung across the crest of the dome. Among the neatly stacked material he found several repair panels, self-adhering and flexible. They were used to make quick, temporary patches of small air leaks.

Each panel was roughly four feet square. He selected one, handling it easily in the light gravity, and checked the adhesive strips along the edges to make certain they weren't activated. The last thing he wanted was for the panel to stick.

Moving carefully along the catwalk he leaned over the side until he had a clear view of the gunman prowling beneath. Then he raised the panel and heaved it toward the Greenhouse. It struck the roof and began to slide down the side of the transparent dome.

Inside the Greenhouse the gunman heard the scraping noise overhead, whirled and adjusted his weapon in the same motion. He was extremely fast. A single shot was fired at the dark silhouette sliding across his sights and then he was racing for the hatch as escaping air began to whistle through the tiny hole.

O'Niel put all his strength behind his next throw. The heavy tank of liquid sealant struck the bullet hole sharply. The impact on the already weakened glass panel was devastating.

The gunman's hand reached for the hatchway handle a second too late. Above, the tank of sealant shattered the entire weakened panel. The whistle of escaping atmosphere became thunder.

Plants, troughs, lights, and writhing water pipes exploded out through the gap in the dome roof as O'Niel crouched down against the protective metal of the catwalk. Seconds later the rest of the interdependent panels followed, sending a shower of glass skyward. Jupiter light turned the glistening fragments orange and yellow.

Mixed in with the ruined plants and machinery was the body of the second gunman, the bones of his hand still outstretched toward the forever unattainable hatchcover.

O'Niel allowed himself to collapse on the catwalk, exhausted, sore, and relieved.

Ballard had finished filling his tanks and entered the waiting elevator.

Lazarus was still fooling with the surveillance monitors, searching for O'Niel, when one of the monitors unexpectedly showed her Ballard entering his elevator. She stared at the screen, her hands trembling.

More than anything she was angry at herself. A doctor's hands shouldn't shake, no matter how desperate the circumstances. And a doctor's perception of the human condition should be better.

She had no way of identifying O'Niel's suit frequency. It had been selected by the suit's original owner. There were hundreds of possible combinations. Her chances of hitting it as she ran through the spectrum of audio possibilities were next to impossible.

Still shaking she made a hasty examination of the complex security console. There was a panel marked EMERGENCY WARNING SYSTEM. Two columns, one for internal, one for Outside.

Her eyes ran down the long list of buttons. There was a warning light for every section of the mine. She found the line for Elevators, pushed the one alongside the legend NUMBER SEVEN.

A red and blue strobe light began flashing above the elevator shaft near the power station feeds. O'Niel was sitting up now, but his back was to the lift shaft and he didn't see the light. Nor was it likely to attract his attention. The sky around the mine was always full of flashing lights.

Ballard's elevator was on its way up. He had the riot gun out and ready. He hadn't bothered to check it because O'Niel had done that earlier.

Lazarus hit the console several times with a tiny fist, her lips tightly clenched. Then she ran from the room.

The elevator slowed, stopped. The doors opened and Ballard stepped out, looked around. He was as high as it was possible to get within the mine complex without flying. Far below and to the right was the shuttle dock, vapor rising from around it.

O'Niel still sat slumped on the catwalk, his back to the elevator and the urgently flashing strobe. Time to move, he thought. There was one more thing he had to do. He started to rise and turn toward the elevator shaft.

Tracers whizzed silently around him. Some struck the solar collectors and their transfer cables and boxes. Blue sparks fled into nothingness and electric arcs jumped nervously in all directions.

Only the tracers gave O'Niel reason to react. If whoever was firing them had stopped long enough to have thought to remove them he could have sat patiently wherever he was and fired away until O'Niel was hit. In the absence of sound the glow of the tracers gave the gunman's presence and approximate location away.

Now flattened out on the catwalk O'Niel could see the flashing security light above the elevator shaft and knew that someone had used it to come after him. He wondered momentarily who had activated the warning light, then silently blessed Lazarus, wherever she was. He started crawling.

Ballard squinted into the darkness and harsh reflections from the buildings beyond, unable to tell whether O'Niel was down because he'd been hit or because he'd dodged in time. He started toward the nearest solar collector. They offered the only escape route and cover, and O'Niel was sure to head in that direction if he could still move.

O'Niel couldn't see his pursuer yet, but he knew from the angle of the tracers that he was somewhere below. He also knew that whoever it was he wouldn't stay in one place for long. Keeping low he headed for one of the enormous panels, wishing desperately for a weapon.

Ballard reached a point below the catwalk and hesitated. There was a ladder nearby but if O'Niel planned any kind of ambush he'd be expecting his pursuers to ascend that way. Each solar collector had a maintenance ridge running along its upper surface. Ballard chose one and started climbing upward. The sight of the ruined Greenhouse made him doubly cautious. Unlike the two presumably dead hired guns, he knew O'Niel well enough to know he was capable of anything.

The Marshal stayed on the catwalk, crawling past the point where the ladder intersected it from below and continued on. He could sense the nearness of the transformers below. His hair tingled inside the helmet. Blue arcs rippled across the surface of the collectors as energy was transferred from the sun to special cells to the collector conduits.

Ballard continued to climb the maintenance ridge on the panel below the catwalk, assuming the Marshal was still somewhere on the catwalk behind him. He was half right.

Over a short distance a frightened man can crawl almost as fast as he can walk. O'Niel was just above Ballard. The catwalk, barely four feet wide, provided little room to hide, but O'Neil had to risk a look over the side. Ballard's helmet indicated he was still searching the section of catwalk at which he'd first fired.

O'Niel waited until the other man was directly below. Then he swung himself over the catwalk railing and fell straight down, kicking violently in the low gravity. Ballard was just starting to turn when O'Niel's foot caught the side of his helmet.

The deputy reeled forward, propelled by the force of the kick. The riot gun flew out of his hands and the impact stunned him. It also sent O'Niel drifting backward. He cursed himself for kicking too hard as he flailed for a grip. There was nothing within reach and he tumbled lazily over the side of the collector.

The gun preceded both bodies downward,

striking the side of the tilted panel. It inter-sected the highly charged field and sparks flared violently in the emptiness, but faded quickly. So did the gun as it spun off the panel and down into the darkness.

Desperately O'Niel clawed for the ridge run-ning along the edge of the panel, twisting to keep his legs from contacting the charged side. Ballard had fallen down the ridge, now climbed to his feet.

Turning, he saw O'Niel struggling for a foot-hold on the ridge. Recognition passed between them.

Then Ballard lunged forward, trying to kick O'Niel's faceplate in. O'Niel grabbed the man's suit leg. The kicks were slowed by the light gravity. The two men fought silently. Below them lay the power station terminals and the rest of the mine.

Ballard kept lashing out with hands and feet while O'Niel clung to him and the edge of the ridge with equal determination. Finally he gave a desperate yank on the ankle he held and let go with his other hand, using his weight to pull at the deputy.

Ballard overbalanced and went over the side. Both men drifted just past the dangerous-ly crackling panel. They clawed at the vacuum, trying to find something to latch onto besides the charged upper surface of the collector.

O'Niel's swinging hands contacted some-thing solid. His fingers locked around it. He knew it couldn't be part of the charged panel because he'd already be dead. As he stopped falling he saw that it was one of the struts supporting the upper row of collectors.

Ballard had grabbed onto the same strut. They fought each other as they climbed onto the narrow support.

O'Niel's damaged shoulder was finally beginning to claim its due. He couldn't hold on with both arms anymore. Ballard leaned at him, started to pry the one remaining hand from the strut. O'Niel didn't have the strength both to continue fighting and to hold on.

He felt his fingers being inexorably pried loose. Using his free hand he reached around toward Ballard's back.

The deputy was concentrating on keeping his legs locked around the strut while using both hands to pull O'Niel's fingers away from the metal. He'd almost succeeded when O'Niel's free hand contacted what it had been groping for, which was not another saving grip on Ballard's body but the manual shut-off valve on the man's air regulator. O'Niel gave it a violent twist.

Ballard drew a breath, only it wasn't there. He started to choke. Letting go of O'Niel he fumbled at his back for the closed valve.

As O'Niel regained his grasp on the strut with both hands he kicked up and out. Both of Ballard's hands were working at his back and the kick was unopposed. The blow wasn't as forceful as O'Niel would have liked, but it was sufficient to send the disconcerted, gasping deputy back and sideways. He fell.

His right foot struck the surface of the lower collector panel. There was a geyser of blue-white sparks, silent fireworks in the dark sky. Ballard's body contorted as the charge passed through him. Then his back contacted the pan-

el and there was a storm of energy that made
the first look insignificant.

Within the power station terminal far below
a readout suddenly dropped a number of ergs.
The drop was so brief the technician on duty
never noticed it.

Ballard slid slowly down the sloping panel,
shimmering with the power that was surging
through him, already dead from that first slight
contact.

Then he tumbled over the edge and started
the long fall. There was a pause until he
reached the transformers. A brief flash of flame
showed where his stiff body struck, where
channeled energy was detoured long enough to
reduce it to ashes.

O'Niel stared downward, his arms draped
tightly around the strut. The fire below faded
quickly as the last of the combustible material
that had been Ballard was reduced to cinders.
The Marshal didn't care if yet another unexpected assassin might be prowling somewhere
overhead. He was dead tired.

Which was, he reflected as he closed his
eyes, much better than being dead, period . . . .

Lazarus moped around the Club. It was a
place she rarely visited, more alien to her than
the surface of Io. On the occasions when she
chose to get drunk she did so in the privacy of
the hospital. She drew curious stares and muffled comments from those who recognized her.
Otherwise no one paid her the least attention.
The usual hectic, noisy crowd jostled her as it
swirled around the bar. The booths near the

back were filled and the suspended dancers stomped sweatily to the blare of the music pouring from the concealed speakers.

A figure appeared in the front entrance. Its shoulder was heavily bandaged and the cloth was stained black. The man's face was bruised and dirty. He just stood there in the doorway, watching, searching.

It was several seconds before the patrons milling around the entrance noticed O'Niel. They stopped talking, drinks halted halfway to mouths. The silence spread like a wave across the room, rolling over tables and dancers to finally crest against the bar. The professional dancers stopped moving in their cylinders, breathing hard, sweat pouring down their nearly nude bodies as they stared at the entrance.

Lazarus had turned with the others. When she saw who had struck the silence, she smiled.

Sheppard was sitting in his usual chair, at his usual table. He frowned at the sudden absence of sound. It was never, never completely quiet in the Club.

He stood and followed the other looks. When he recognized the Marshal his mouth opened as wide as his eyes.

O'Niel started across the room toward the General Manager, moving with obvious pain, his progress slow. He passed the silent workers at the bar and seated at their tables without looking anywhere but straight ahead.

It took a long time but eventually he was standing in front of Sheppard. The Manager said nothing, for once, speechless.

"Sheppard . . . ." O'Niel hesitated. He shook

his head at nothing in particular. "Oh . . . fuck it."

The punch knocked the General Manager across the table and back into the curtains shielding a booth. They came down under his weight, burying him.

O'Niel sighed, his expression unreadable, and turned. He strode out of the Club with half a thousand eyes fastened to his back. He didn't notice them because they didn't exist.

Gradually conversation resumed, subdued and self-conscious.

Lazarus turned to one of the dazed bartenders. "Bourbon and soda, fatso, and snap it up. I've got some catching up to do."

O'Niel walked into the squad room. The next shift was waiting there, wondering what had happened to Ballard. There was some whispering when they saw O'Niel. He ignored them utterly. None had the temerity to speak. After awhile, they slowly filed out of the room and left him alone.

The keyboard was waiting. He stared thoughtfully at the activated screens, then typed briskly.

MESSAGE TO O'NIEL, CAROL G. — STATION GREEN. FROM O'NIEL, W.T. — IO.

ARRIVING IN TIME FOR FLIGHT. KEEP TICKET WARM. JOB DONE. KISS PAUL FOR ME. LOOKING FORWARD TO SLEEPING WITH YOU FOR A YEAR.

O'NIEL, W.T. — END TRANSMISSION.

He spent another hour alone in the office, programming a chip. When he was through he deposited it in a receiving slot in the front of the console.

Then he rose and walked out of the office for the last time .....

Epilogue

The chip entered a security transmitter. The transmitter broke down the contents of the chip into a regularized pattern of electrical impulses which were metamorphosed into a stream of photons and shipped out across the vacuum.

Relay stations picked up the stream, powerful lasers at each, regenerating the message and casting it onward through the void. Eventually the stream arrived at a security receiver, was sucked in and rearranged as electrical impulses.

The impulses were automatically fed into a computer which decoded them. It was quite a long message, very explicit, and detailed. People arrived to study the re-integrated patterns. They began to move in response, slower than the impulses but quickly nonetheless.

Circuitry flashed. New patterns were shunted to and fro around the solar system. Many people became aware of them. Those so apprised reacted excitedly, but for very different reasons.

The Outland Transport was cutting the orbit of the asteroids when it was passed in space by a succession of tight-beam transmissions jumping from one booster station to the next.

Eventually this fresh stream of information arrived at the central Security Depot on Station Green, the center for Trans-Jovian operations.

The receiver there performed the magic of turning light into electric pulses which activated a computer, which activated a screen printer, which informed the uniformed people gazing at it of certain interesting facts.

ANALYSIS OF DATA PROVIDED BY O'NIEL, W.T., MARSHAL RETIRED. LAST DUTY POST IO, CON-AMALGAMATED MINE.

RESULTS

1) RECOMMEND TRANSFER LAZARUS, MARIAN L. DR. IO INFIRMARY TO STAFF, COPERNICUS GENERAL, LUNA.

2) INDICTMENT OF FOLLOWING, MULTIPLE CHARGES, WARRANTS ISSUED FOR:

SHEPPARD, MARK B.—IO
APUNRA, KURAT—GANYMEDE
VELAR, GWEN L.—STATION GREEN
JURGENSON, KNUT S. — COPENHA-
GEN, NORTH EUROPE, EARTH
MENDOZA, JORGE X. . . . .

It was a very long list, and almost as satisfying to the men and women who watched it unfold on Station Green as was the warmth of the woman O'Niel held tightly next to him in the bed on board the transport . . . .

A MIND-BENDING FORAY INTO ADVENTURE AND DANGER!

FALSE DAWN
by Chelsea Quinn Yarbro   (90-077, $1.95)

In the mountains neither of them stood a chance alone. Out of desperation, Thea, the grotesque mutant, and Evan, the mutilated pirate set off together to seek a haven . . . trusting each other because they must. A spellbinding novel of a defiant love illuminating the New Dark Ages of the 21st century.

STRANGE WINE
by Harlan Ellison   (91-946, $2.50)

Fifteen new stories from the nightside of the world by one of the most original and entertaining short-story writers in America today. Discover among these previously uncollected tales the spirits of executed Nazi war criminals, gremlins, a murderess escaped from hell, and other chilling, thought provoking tales.

TITLES BY KARL EDWARD WAGNER

BLOODSTONE
by Karl Edward Wagner   (90-139, $1.95)

Kane—the Mystic Swordsman becomes the living link with the awesome power of a vanished super-race. Now Kane, whose bloody sword has slashed and killed for the glory of other rulers can scheme to rule the Earth—himself!

DARK CRUSADE
by Karl Edward Wagner   (90-021, $1.95)

Kane—the Mystic Swordsman battles the prophet of an ancient cult of evil that began before the birth of man. Join in on this adventure as Kane commands an army against the power of primeval black sorcery for one purpose alone—He intends to rule the Earth!

DARKNESS WEAVES
by Karl Edward Wagner   (89-589, $1.95)

In this adventure Kane, the Mystic Swordsman leads the avenging forces of an island empress, a ravaged ruler bent on bitter revenge. Only he can deliver the vengeance she has devised in her knowledge of black magic and in her power to unleash the demons of the deep.

THE BEST OF SCIENCE FROM WARNER BOOKS

SHUTTLE
by Robert M. Powers (95-331, $2.75)

Join the crew of space shuttle *Columbia* as they prepare to take the first step into the twenty-first century. Step aboard the world's first reusable space vehicle with science writer Robert M. Powers for a cockpit view of a launch, orbit, re-entry, and return to earth. The shuttle system is the key to unlocking the next era of technology and the forerunner of space transportation systems of tomorrow.

PROCEEDINGS OF THE FIRST INTERNATIONAL UFO CONGRESS
compiled and edited by Curtis G. Fuller (95-159, $2.75)

From the experts . . . a sober look at the fantastical. After thirty years of research, eye-witness reports, hysteria, hoax and cover-up, what do we *really* know about the UFO phenomenon? To answer this fascinating question, *Fate* magazine sponsored the first conference of the world's foremost authorities and witnesses. Here are their extraordinary findings.

PLANETARY ENCOUNTERS
by Robert M. Powers (93-330, $2.95)

PLANETARY ENCOUNTERS covers the expeditions of robot vehicles—the mechanical extensions of man's senses. In vivid, non-technical language, this book digests all of what is known about past missions and projects the possibilities for the next 20 years; the exploration and mapping of the entire solar system and the turning of the probes toward deep space and beyond. WINNER, *National Aviation/Space Writers Association Award Best Non-fiction Space Book.*

SPACE TREK
by Jerome Clayton Glenn and George S. Robinson (91-122, $2.50)

Floating cities! Solar sailboats! Moon mining! Electronic Sex! These were the stuff of science fiction dreams but soon they will be the realities of science fact. By 1992 there should be ten thousand people working and living in outer space—in an environment complete with trees, birds and rivers. We have the means. But what are the risks to the pioneers? Who will be the first to go? What are the urgent reasons for us to undertake such a vast project? The answers are here in this blueprint for a new era—SPACE TREK.

GREAT SCIENCE FICTION
FROM WARNER...

ALIEN
by Alan Dean Foster   (82-977, $2.25)
Astronauts encounter an awesome galactic horror on a distant planet. But it is only when they take off again that the real horror begins. For the alien is now within the ship, within the crew itself. And a classic deathtrap suspense begins.

WHEN WORLDS COLLIDE
by Philip Wylie and Edwin Balmer   (92-812, $2.25)
When the extinction of Earth is near, scientists build rocket ships to evacuate a chosen few to a new planet. But the secret leaks out and touches off a savage struggle among the world's most powerful men for the million-to-one chance of survival.

AFTER WORLDS COLLIDE
by Philip Wylie and Edwin Balmer   (92-813, $2.25)
When the group of survivors from Earth landed on Bronson Beta, they expected absolute desolation. But the Earth people found a breathtakingly beautiful city encased in a hugh metal bubble, filled with food for a lifetime but with no trace either of life—or death. Then the humans learned that they were not alone on Bronson Beta . . .

WARNER BOOKS
P.O. Box 690
New York, N.Y. 10019

Please send me the books I have selected. Enclose check or money order only, no cash please. Plus 50¢ per order and 20¢ per copy to cover postage and handling. N.Y. State and California residents add applicable sales tax.

Please allow 4 weeks for delivery.

_____ Please send me your free
mail order catalog

_____ Please send me your free
Romance books catalog

Name_____

Address_____

City_____

State_____ Zip_____